PLAYING WITH FIRE

FIREHOUSE FOURTEEN
BOOK 2

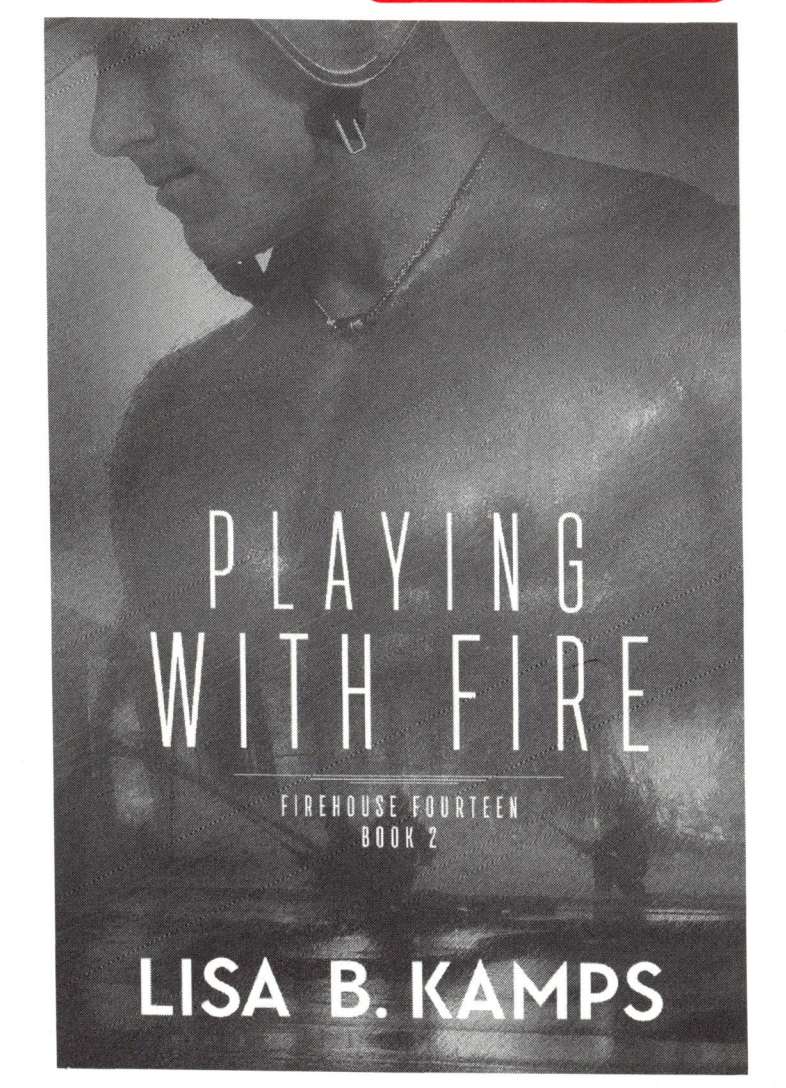

LISA B. KAMPS

Lisa B. Kamps

Playing With Fire
Firehouse Fourteen Book 2

Lisa B. Kamps

PLAYING WITH FIRE

PLAYING WITH FIRE

PLAYING WITH FIRE
Copyright © 2016 by Elizabeth Belbot Kamps

All rights reserved. Except for use in any review, the reproduction or utilization of this work in whole or in part in any form by any electronic, mechanical or other means, now known or hereafter invented, including xerography, photocopying and recording, or in any information storage or retrieval system, is forbidden without the express written permission of the author.

All characters in this book have no existence outside the imagination of the author and have no relation to anyone bearing the same name or names, living or dead. This book is a work of fiction and any resemblance to any individual, place, business, or event is purely coincidental.

Cover and logo design by Jay Aheer of Simply Defined Art
http://www.jayscoversbydesign.com/

Lisa B. Kamps

All rights reserved.
ISBN: 1532834764
ISBN-13: 978-1532834769

PLAYING WITH FIRE

Lisa B. Kamps

DEDICATION

For the 71st Recruit Class,
Baltimore County Fire Department.
It's been more than thirty years since "The Biggest
and the Best" graduated.
It's been one hell of a ride, guys!

PLAYING WITH FIRE

Contents

Title Page iii
Copyright v
Dedicatiom ix
Other titles by this author xv

Chapter One 17
Chapter Two 24
Chapter Three 30
Chapter Four 35
Chapter Five 42
Chapter Six 47
Chapter Seven 55
Chapter Eight 66
Chapter Nine 74
Chapter Ten 81
Chapter Eleven 92
Chapter Twelve 99
Chapter Thirteen 111
Chapter Fourteen 116
Chapter Fifteen 124
Chapter Sixteen 134
Chapter Seventeen 143
Chapter Eighteen 152
Chapter Nineteen 157
Chapter Twenty 166
Chapter Twenty-One 174
Chapter Twenty-Two 185
Chapter Twenty-Three 191
Chapter Twenty-Four 204

Chapter Twenty-Five 211
Chapter Twenty-Six 218
Chapter Twenty-Seven 226
Chapter Twenty-Eight 236
Chapter Twenty-Nine 243
Chapter Thirty 251
Chapter Thirty-One 259
Chapter Thirty-Two 267
Chapter Thirty-Three 274
Chapter Thirty-Four 282

ABOUT THE AUTHOR 291

# PLAYING WITH FIRE

Lisa B. Kamps

Other titles by this author

THE BALTIMORE BANNERS

Crossing The Line, Book 1
Game Over, Book 2
Blue Ribbon Summer, Book 3
Body Check, Book 4
Break Away, Book 5
Playmaker (A Baltimore Banners Intermission novella)
Delay of Game, Book 6
Shoot Out, Book 7
The Baltimore Banners 1st Period Trilogy (Books 1-3)

FIREHOUSE FOURTEEN

Once Burned, Book 1
Playing With Fire, Book 2
Breaking Protocol, Book 3

STAND-ALONE TITLES

Emeralds and Gold: A Treasury of Irish Short Stories
(anthology)
Finding Dr. Right, Silhouette Special Edition
Time To Heal

Lisa B. Kamps

Chapter One

Music from an old jukebox filled the bar, loud enough to be heard over the noise of the crowd that filled Duffy's. Jay Moore took a swig of beer from the sweaty bottle then sat it on the edge of the stained pool table. He leaned over, eyeing his shot and knowing he was going to miss. He closed his eyes against the low throb of the headache at the base of his skull, pulled back his stick, then shoved it forward. The cue ball slid across the green and hit the two ball with a loud clack before shooting to the left and dropping into the corner pocket.

"Shit." Jay shook his head and took another swig of beer as several of his coworkers teased him.

"Oh, nice one, Moore. For me. Now cough up." His lieutenant, Pete Miller, slapped him on the back then held his hand out, palm up, waiting. Jay muttered to himself and pulled out his wallet, rifling through the bills until he found a twenty and slammed it into Pete's outstretched hand.

Dave Warren, the paramedic from their shift,

jokingly pushed him out of the way so he could rack the balls for the next game. "You playing next?"

"No, I'm done. You guys are taking me broke." Jay walked around the table and placed his stick in the rack then raised his arms above his head and stretched. Pete walked by, slapping him in the stomach then laughing at Jay's groan.

"Yeah, your game is definitely off tonight. Not that we're complaining!" Pete laughed then motioned his head toward the bar. "You know the rules. Loser gets next round."

"None for me." Dave shook his head before Jay could head to the bar. "I'm working call back tomorrow."

"Again? Shit, with all that overtime, you should be the one buying."

"Don't complain. If you actually worked for a living instead of being a lazy ass firefighter, you could be raking in the overtime, too."

Jay and Pete both turned to him with identical looks of horror on their faces.

"Oh, hell no."

"Yeah, what Pete said." Jay laughed and moved around the table, leaving his friends behind as he walked to the bar. He wedged his foot into the bottom rail of a stool and pulled it out, then lifted himself into it and leaned forward, resting his arms on the varnished surface of the bar. He grimaced at the stickiness under one elbow and immediately lifted it, looking around for a napkin. A damp rag landed in front of him with a soggy plop and he grabbed it without looking up, using it to wipe his elbows first, then the bar in front of him. He neatly folded the rag then held it out to the girl who appeared in front of him.

"Thanks Ang. Two beers when you get the chance."

"Yeah, sure."

Something in the girl's tone caught his attention and he finally looked up, surprised to see a frown on her face. "What's wrong kiddo?"

"You, too? You can just stop it whenever." Angie gave him a quick hard look then moved to the other side of the bar, leaning over into the cooler and coming up with two bottles. Jay watched as she reached into the back pocket of her tight jeans and pulled out a bottle opener before quickly snapping the tops off both bottles. His eyes were focused on her shapely ass for a full thirty seconds before he realized where he was looking. He turned his head away and inwardly groaned.

What the hell was he doing? He needed to get his head examined for even thinking about looking at Angie. He turned around and glanced back at the pool table, thankful that Dave had his back turned to the bar. He didn't want to think what his friend would do if he caught him ogling his baby sister.

Yeah, that wouldn't go over really well.

And what the hell was he doing looking, anyway?

Angie put the bottles in front of Jay with a loud thunk then grabbed the rag and started wiping down the bar, her knuckles nearly white with the grip she had on it. Jay frowned then studied her face, noticing the tension in the set of her shoulders and the wariness etched at the corners of her eyes.

"Hey. You okay?" Jay pitched his voice low enough that nobody else would be able to hear him. At first he thought that maybe he had spoken too quietly, because Angie didn't answer him. But she finally looked up from scrubbing the bar long enough to give him a scowl.

"I'm fine."

"You sure?"

She paused before quickly glancing at the two guys at the far end of the bar, then went back to attacking the finish on the counter. "I'm fine."

Jay grabbed his bottle and lifted it to his mouth, taking his time as he quietly studied the two guys she had glanced at. He figured they were around Angie's age, probably just old enough to be in here drinking, maybe only recently turned twenty-one. They looked so much younger than his thirty years. Watching them, sitting there in their designer shorts and baggy button down shirts, laughing too loudly, Jay suddenly felt old. Much older. He sighed and put his beer back on the counter, then leaned forward.

"They giving you a hard time?"

Angie finally stopped rubbing at the clean bar counter and tossed the rag into a bucket behind her. She glanced over at the two guys then turned back to face Jay with a grimace. She reached up and tucked a strand of dark hair behind her ear then slowly shook her head.

"No. The one guy's my ex, that's all."

"Hm." Jay didn't know what else to say, because a sudden flare of some unknown emotion flashed through him. Probably a protective streak. He had known Angie for a couple of years. And she was Dave's kid sister. Of course he was going to be protective.

And Christ, he needed to get away, now, before he looked too deeply into whatever the hell had just happened. He grabbed both bottles and stood up. "Well, you know where to find me—us—if they give you any trouble."

Angie just looked at him, her dark brown eyes clear as she watched him. A bright smile suddenly lit her face, transforming the features into something less angelic and sultrier than they had a right to be. Jay tried to take a step back, his leg colliding with the stool as she reached out and laid a hand on his arm, gently squeezing.

"Thanks Jay, I appreciate it."

"Yeah. No problem." He swallowed then forced a smile. "Kiddo."

He quickly turned away, surprised by the flash of disappointment that crossed her face when he called her 'kiddo'. But he would not think about that. Hell no.

What the hell was wrong with him?

He made his way back to the pool table and handed a beer to Pete, making sure to keep his back to the bar. He did not need to be watching Angie. No way in hell.

"Is she okay?"

Jay jumped in surprise when he noticed Dave standing next to him, his attention focused on the bar behind him.

"Who?"

"My sister. You know, the one you were just talking to?"

"Oh. Yeah. Yeah, she's fine. Why?"

"Because that punk asshole is her ex-boyfriend and I don't like the fact that he's in here. I'm tempted to go over and punch him in the face just on principle."

"Damn, Dave, calm down." Pete placed a restraining hand on Dave's shoulder, as if to stop him from doing anything stupid. Jay took another sip of beer and kept his mouth shut.

"She's my sister, asshole."

"Yeah, but she's a big girl. She just turned twenty-four, she can handle herself."

Jay choked on the swallow of beer, coughing hard enough that both men turned and looked at him. He waved away their concern then brushed a splash of beer from his shirt.

Twenty-four? Angie was twenty-four? When the hell had that happened?

"I don't care how old she is, she's still my sister." Dave shrugged Pete's hand from his shoulder then placed his cue stick back in the rack. He tossed another look toward the end of the bar then shook his head. "I have to get going. Are you two going to be here awhile, make sure she gets out okay? I don't like the idea of her closing up by herself with those two guys here."

"Yeah, one of us will stay, don't worry. We'll make sure nothing happens to Angie." Pete laughed, reassuring Dave even though he was rolling his eyes at the same time. Jay looked over at him, his expression no doubt clearly asking Pete what the hell he was talking about.

Dave didn't comment, just nodded then moved to the bar, leaning over to say something to Angie. Her expression of annoyance was clear and almost comical, and Jay felt himself smile in reaction. Her eyes locked with his and she raised her brows in his direction. Jay's smile faded and he quickly turned his back to her, wondering again what the hell was wrong with him.

He needed to find a date. A one-night encounter. Hell, something. But he had been on a strike-out streak for the last six months, probably because he had lost interest in the entire dating scene. He was tired of the games, tired of the acting, tired of the drama.

Just tired, period.

Which was his problem tonight, it had to be.

Jay looked over at Pete, who was watching him expectantly. He shook his head. "Sorry, didn't catch that."

"I said, can you stay and watch out for Angie? I need to get ready to go myself."

"Why the hell for? It's still early."

"Because I still feel like shit, trying to get rid of this damn cold. The beer doesn't even taste good anymore." Pete's expression was one of annoyance, and Jay felt himself smile. God forbid the beer didn't taste good.

"Yeah, I got it."

"Thanks, I owe you. Even though I still say Dave's overreacting. He needs to loosen the reins. She's a grown woman, for crying out loud."

"Yeah, but she's his sister. And you know how he gets."

"True. And if I had a sister as cute as Angie, I'd probably act like an even bigger ass than he does. Anyway, I'm out of here. See you first day in." Pete gave him a small salute then turned around and left, leaving Jay standing next to the pool table by himself.

And wondering what the hell he had just agreed to.

Two hours later, and he was still wondering the

same thing. Angie had called last call and the bar was empty except for him and the two guys at the end. He had taken turns watching them and talking to Angie since Pete and Dave had left.

Talking to Angie had definitely been more fun, especially when one of the guys kept tossing him dirty looks all night. Jay felt himself smile. Let him think they were a couple. If that stopped them from coming in and giving Angie a hard time, then he was all for it.

He had learned from her that Todd—a small shudder went through Jay when he learned the guy's name—and she had dated for a few weeks, and that she broke it off over three months ago.

Because the guy was immature and egotistical. Yeah, Jay had picked up on that thirty seconds after seeing the guy, but he didn't tell Angie that.

As to why Todd and his friend were here, Angie didn't know. She hadn't bothered talking to either of them except for taking their orders and ringing them up.

Jay watched the two of them now, narrowing his eyes in their direction as they tossed some bills on the counter and finally left. Angie walked over and grabbed the money, staring down at it with a scowl.

"I can't believe those assholes!" She walked over to the register and rang up the sale, slamming the drawer closed after placing the bills inside.

"Everything okay?"

"Yeah. They stiffed me on the tip. No idea why I'm surprised." She reached behind her and bunched her hair in one fist, pulling it off her neck as she let out a deep breath. She rolled her head from one side to the next, then gave a short laugh and faced Jay. "I really shouldn't be surprised. Anyway, I'm almost done here. You don't have to wait around."

"I'll wait and walk you out."

"Seriously, Jay, you don't have to. I don't even know why you stayed."

"Because Dave asked me to watch over you."

"Of course he did. Great." She shook her head and came around the bar, turning off lights as she went. "You know, I've been working here for almost a year. I've closed by myself before, it's not a big deal."

"Yeah, but—"

"I'm a grown woman, Jay. I can take care of myself. You don't need to babysit me."

Jay closed his mouth against the comment he was going to make, sensing that Angie was suddenly in a foul mood. But maybe it wasn't so sudden, since he had detected something wrong about her a few hours ago. He had thought that whatever was wrong, she had gotten over it.

Apparently not.

So he didn't say anything, just walked beside her as they left the bar and waited for her to lock up. She looked over her shoulder at him, the neon light from the sign over the door casting her oval face in shades of pink and blue. Her dark eyes shone in the light as she studied him, their gaze clear but unreadable. She finally muttered something to herself and turned the key in the lock, pulling on the door to make sure it was locked.

"Okay, I'm done. You can go now."

"I'll walk you to your car."

Angie muttered something again then walked through the parking lot, the gravel crunching beneath her feet. Jay fell into step behind her, not stopping until she reached her car. He honestly had no idea why she seemed irritated, since her car was parked right next to his truck.

She tossed another look at him over her shoulder, shook her head, then opened the door of her car. "Good night Jay."

"Good night. Drive safe."

He heard her mutter something that sounded suspiciously like a curse before she slammed the door shut, safely sealing her inside the little car. Jay shook his head again, still wondering about her mood, then walked over to his truck and climbed inside. He started the ignition and felt a kick of childish excitement at the rumbling of the engine before leaning forward and turning down the volume of the stereo. He hit the power button and lowered the window, looking over at Angie and waiting for her to pull out in front of him.

She was sitting in the front seat, her hand turning the key in the ignition. He watched her shake her head then pound her fist against the steering wheel in frustration.

With a sigh, he killed the engine on the truck then climbed out. He motioned for her to pop the hood on her car, then waited a full minute before he heard the latch release.

"Go ahead and try again." He leaned forward, listening as she turned the key.

Click click click, grind.
Click click. Grind.
Click.
Silence.

"Do you think it's the battery?" Angie's voice

came from beside him but he didn't bother to turn and face her. He merely shook his head and leaned closer to the engine, shaking some wires, looking to make sure there weren't any loose connections.

"Try it again." He waited for her to get back into the car, then leaned closer to listen.

Click.

Silence.

Jay shook his head then slammed the hood shut. Angie leaned out the window, her lower lip pulled between her teeth as she watched him walk around the side of the car. "Is it the battery? Do you have cables?"

"I think it's the alternator. Jump start won't work. When's the last time you had the car serviced?"

Silence greeted his question and he didn't bother to say anything in response. She probably hadn't had the car serviced. Jay didn't understand why Dave hadn't made sure his own sister's car was working right.

"C'mon, I'll give you a lift home. We'll get it fixed in the morning." Jay opened the door for her, waiting for her to get out and telling himself that his use of the word 'we' meant absolutely nothing.

"But I'm working at the clinic tomorrow as part of my internship. I can't miss it!"

"Internship?"

"Yeah, for vet school."

"Can't Dave take you?" Even as he asked, he knew the answer. No, Dave couldn't take her, because Dave was working call back. Jay sighed and ran one hand through his short hair as Angie finally climbed out of the car. "Never mind. I'll take you then come back and work on the car. What time do you have to be there?"

"Nine. And I can't let you do that. It's too far for you to drive to our place, then back home, then back again. It's too much, Jay."

Whether it was or wasn't didn't matter because he had already offered. And it wasn't like he had anything else planned for tomorrow—today—anyway. "Not a problem, really. C'mon, let's go."

But Angie was shaking her head and leaning into the backseat, her shapely ass outlined by the worn faded denim of her jeans. Jay closed his eyes and swallowed, once again calling himself a fool for noticing.

"I have a better idea. I can just crash at your place, and you can drop me off in the morning. I already have everything I need right here." She held up a full backpack and offered him a bright smile before slamming the door shut and brushing by him.

And no, he hadn't imagined her literally brushing by him, the softness of her cotton shirt—the fullness of one soft breast—against his chest as she stepped around him.

What the hell? He was losing his mind. It had to have been an accident.

And he was scum for noticing, scum for taking even a split-second pleasure at the contact.

Then her words finally registered and he opened his mouth to say no, that it was completely inappropriate for her to even think about crashing at his place. But it was too late, because she had already climbed into the passenger seat of his truck, watching him with a bright smile on her face.

Jay didn't bother to hide his groan as he climbed in after her, his mind going full speed ahead, trying to find a way to tell her that she was not, no way in hell, crashing at his place.

Chapter Two

"Thanks Jay, you have no idea how much I appreciate this." Angie tossed him a smile as she walked into the bathroom, closing the door behind her.

He didn't move.

In fact, he hadn't moved from the spot just inside the front door of his apartment for the last five minutes. His feet had been frozen in place ever since they walked inside. Not just his feet; his voice and, quite apparently, his mind were also frozen.

Just what the hell did he think he was doing? Fuck. Okay, he was making more out of this than it really was. She was just crashing on the sofa for the night, that was all. Nothing else. Wouldn't be the first time one of his buddies crashed on his sofa.

Except Angie wasn't one of his buddies. No, she was Dave's sister. His *friend's* sister. His friend's *baby* sister.

Which didn't change anything. She was simply crashing, that was all.

Except he was having a hard time forgetting about their drive here from the bar. She had been leaning too close to him, her hand or arm brushing against him too frequently. And when she had leaned over in her enthusiasm to check out the various controls on the steering wheel of the new truck, he had been pretty sure that her chest had been brushing against his arm.

In fact, if it had been anyone else, Jay would swear that Angie had actually been flirting with him.

Flirting.

With him.

And if it had been anyone else, he would have flirted back, would already be wooing her into his bed.

But she wasn't anyone else. She was Dave's *baby sister*.

Holy shit, he needed somebody to tell him he had been imagining things. Because another thing he had noticed on the way home was that Angie most definitely was not a kid.

Far from it.

And she had been flirting. With him.

Shit. He really, really needed someone to tell him he was imagining things. Only it was almost three o'clock in the morning and there wasn't anyone he could call right now.

That insane thought snapped him out of his frozen state and he mentally kicked himself. He was being an ass. He was thirty years old, he knew how to control himself. He didn't need to talk to anyone. Hell, he really did have morals, and those included *not* panting after his friend's sister.

With that thought firmly in mind, he made a bee

line down the short hall to his bedroom and pulled open the closet. A few spare pillows and extra blankets were on the top shelf, just for those occasions when anyone happened to crash on his sofa.

He stepped into the closet and reached for a pillow, telling himself again that he really needed to look into getting a house or something. Maybe he would start looking this week, it was past time. Satisfied with that plan, he reached up to grab a blanket then turned.

And bumped straight into Angie. She took a step back, her nervous laugh ringing in his ears and doing something funny to his gut.

"Oops, sorry."

Jay got a good look at her and felt his mouth go dry. His grip slipped on the pillow and blanket and they fell to the floor, but he made no move to pick them up. He couldn't, he was too busy staring at Angie.

She stood in front of him like some adolescent's wet dream, dressed in a pair of loose flannel boxers that were entirely too short. The soft material barely covered the tops of her thighs, showing off the length of her toned tanned legs.

Jay tried to swallow as his eyes moved from those shapely legs up, taking in the hint of flat toned stomach that peeked out from the hem of her tank shirt.

Her snug, very thin, white tank shirt.

And she wasn't wearing a bra.

He tried telling himself to stop looking. Dammit, she was a kid. Only she wasn't. And his eyes wouldn't listen to his brain because they were still focused on the fullness of those gorgeous breasts pushing against the thin material of the sleep shirt. So thin that he could see the dark outline of her nipples that contrasted with the pale gold of the rest of her skin. As he watched, her nipples hardened, rising to tiny peaks that thrust against the white cotton, as if begging for more attention.

And shit, it was no longer just his eyes that weren't listening to his brain.

Angie laughed again, the sound soft and welcoming as she stepped closer, her eyes never leaving his as she slowly bent over and picked up the pillow and blanket from the floor.

He closed his eyes, desperate to break that contact, calling himself every kind of fool and hoping, please God, that she would just turn around and leave.

But instead of hearing her footsteps retreat from the room, he heard a soft whoosh and even softer thump. He wasn't certain, but he thought that maybe she had tossed the pillow and blanket off to the side. His heart slammed against his chest and he hoped, prayed, he was wrong, prayed that this was not happening.

This couldn't be happening.

Something touched his chest and he knew without seeing that it was Angie's hand. The warmth of her palm through his shirt seared him, branding him, and he swallowed, told himself to move.

Her fingers dipped inside his shirt then slowly worked at the buttons, opening them one by one until his shirt hung open. He swallowed, told himself again to move, dammit, he couldn't be doing this.

Her hands gently caressed his chest, her palms

soft and warm against his bare skin as they explored his body, moving across to his shoulders, down across his flat nipples, down further to his stomach to the waist band of his shorts.

His breath hitched at her touch, and his mind finally came to life. With a sharp inhale, he grabbed her hands and held them still, his eyes now open, his gaze finding and holding hers. The heat in their brown depths seared him but he found the strength to take a step back, her hands still caught in his.

"Angie, what are you doing?" He had meant to sound fierce, to sound in control and let her know that he wasn't going to play whatever game she was playing. But his voice was hoarse, the words coming out in something just above a ragged whisper that completely betrayed the authority he had been hoping to present.

"Did you know that I've had a crush on you for over a year now?"

His stomach clenched at her words. Not just the words, but the husky whisper of her voice.

"Angie." He had no idea what to say, his mind fighting for some sanity in this suddenly crazy situation. And then he couldn't say anything, because her mouth was suddenly on his, her lips soft and moist against his, their touch hesitant.

Any hesitation she may have felt quickly disappeared and she became bolder, darting her tongue out and running the wet tip against his lips, coaxing his own mouth open before he could stop. His tongue met hers, fighting for domination in this, at least.

He must have released her hands at some point because her arms wrapped around his waist, pulling him closer as she molded her body against his. Her soft curves pressed against him and he reached behind her, cupping her ass in his hands and pulling her more tightly against his erection.

A moan escaped her as she thrust her hips against him, and the sound broke the grip of whatever insanity plagued him. He let go of her and pulled away with a groan of his own, trying to take another step back even though she was still holding onto him.

"Angie, stop. We can't do this. I'm not doing this."

"Why?" Her throaty question threw him for a second and he tried to remember exactly why they couldn't do this. He shook his head, trying again to step away.

"Because we can't. You're Dave's sister and we can't—"

"You're not going to tell me you don't want to." A knowing gleam lit her eyes as her hand suddenly dropped from his chest to the front of his shorts. She ran her fingers up the length of his erection then cupped his hard length in her hand, squeezing.

Something snapped inside him at the touch and he had the insane idea that he would fight fire with fire, that he could somehow teach her a lesson. "You're playing with fire, Angie."

"Am I?" One corner of her mouth lifted in a seductively teasing smile, and something snapped in Jay. He had the insane idea to turn the tables, to scare her into realizing that she was going too far.

He cupped the back of her head with one hand and pulled her to him, his mouth slamming on hers in a kiss so fierce there could be no doubt he would conquer her. He caught her breathy moan with his mouth and forced her back against the wall, his free hand skimming the flesh of her stomach before grabbing the hem of her shirt and pulling it up.

He broke the kiss and stared down at her breasts, letting his eyes have their fill before he reached out and rolled one tight nipple between his fingers, lightly squeezing. Angie's head fell back on a low moan and her hips thrust forward, meeting his.

Shit. Shit, shit, this wasn't supposed to be happening.

Jay ignored the warning in his head and leaned down, taking her other nipple in his mouth, teasing, tasting her as his hands skimmed down her sides. His thumbs hooked into the band of her sleep shorts and dragged them down, past her hips, down to her thighs. He rolled his tongue around her nipple one last time then trailed his mouth down her stomach, dropping to his knees in front of her. He opened his eyes and let them feast on the sight of her waist, lower to the barely-there clipped curls between her thighs. He swallowed and looked up, expecting Angie to stare down at him in shock and horror.

Instead she offered him a siren's smile and ran her hand down her neck, down further to cup her breast. He watched, breathless, as she pinched one nipple between her fingers then lowered her hand even more, her fingers spread as they finally came to a stop between her legs. Her smile widened as she thrust her hips forward and slowly opened her legs before his eyes.

Jay swallowed, mesmerized as she spread herself with her index and ring fingers, her middle finger slowly rubbing against her clit. Light from the hall illuminated each touch, each swirl as her hips moved in a slow rhythm, hypnotizing. His throat dried up, his breathing harsh as he watched, helpless to look away as her finger circled her clit, the glint of moisture from her body reflected in the light from the hall.

"Fuck." Jay pushed away and stood up, anger burning bright inside him, pushing away the haze of misplaced passion. Without looking, he grabbed the waistband of her shorts and yanked them up, pulling down on her shirt at the same time. He grabbed her wrist in one hand, reached down and grabbed the blanket and pillow from the floor with his other hand, then pulled her out of his room. She tried tugging against him but he didn't release his hold on her until he reached the sofa.

He threw the blanket and pillow down, then made Angie sit as well. He looked down at her, his breathing still harsh but not as heavy, and ran a hand down his face.

"Fuck," he repeated. He opened his mouth to say something else, then snapped it closed, shaking his head. He turned to go back to his room, thought better of it, stopped and leaned down to place a quick kiss on the top of her head. He didn't miss the look of shock on her face as he turned and stormed back to his room, slamming the door behind him.

And locking it.

He had told her *she* was playing with fire? Yeah, he had never before been so wrong, because he was the one sitting here, burning up.

Fuck.

Chapter Three

Angie sat on the edge of the tub, her brush held loosely in her hand, and seriously considered throwing herself out the bathroom window. There were only two problems with that.

First, she didn't think she could fit through the window.

And second, Jay lived on the ground floor.

Oh God, how was she ever going to face him? She had never ever been so mortified. Ever. And she had never ever done anything like what she did last night. Even now she could feel her face flaming with embarrassment. What had she thought to accomplish? What idiocy had possessed her to come onto Jay like that? And that stunt in his bedroom.

She swallowed a groan and lowered her face into her hands. The thought of going out there and facing him was more than she could bear. It was beyond humiliating, and she still didn't know what had gotten into her.

Yeah, she had been upset because Todd had

shown up at the bar last night. Not really upset, more irritated then anything else. She didn't know why, but suddenly having Jay show her some attention had made her think that maybe she could turn it around, make it look like something else so Todd would leave.

Only she didn't really care what Todd thought, so that excuse didn't really cut it. And then when Jay said he was watching out for her because Dave had asked him to, well, that just irritated her even more.

She had been crushing on Jay for so long, and she was thoroughly tired of him looking at her like she was some kid. The insane idea to flirt with him had seized her as soon as she realized her car wouldn't start. Not that the two had anything to do with each other, but that's how it worked out. So yeah, she thought it would be fun to flirt with him, maybe get him to open his eyes and realize she wasn't a kid.

And yeah, didn't that backfire on her?

Well, no, not really, because she was pretty sure he definitely did *not* think of her as a kid any longer.

No, he probably thought she was some kind of slut now.

What on earth had she been thinking to act that way? To practically throw herself at him and then to try and act like some kind of seductress? And she had actually touched herself, in front of him, begging him to take her. She had never done anything like that before, ever.

And she had absolutely nothing to blame it on, either. She hadn't been drinking, she wasn't on the rebound. The moon wasn't even full.

Angie stood up and tossed all of her things into the back pack, then took care straightening up after herself. Jay was a neat freak, which kind of surprised her, though she wasn't sure why.

And yes, she was procrastinating, because she did not want to go out there and face him.

She moved to the front of the sink and glanced in the mirror, frowning at her reflection before she yanked her hair back and pulled into a pony tail. Her watch beeped the half hour and she sighed. She couldn't stay in Jay's bathroom all day, not when she had to be at the clinic in an hour and a half.

And walking was out of the question, because even she wasn't that energetic. Although maybe a twelve mile run would ease some of her embarrassment.

No, that wouldn't work either. She'd still have to leave the bathroom, which meant she'd still run into Jay. He was up, had already been up when she finally woke up and crawled out from underneath the blanket. Thankfully he was nowhere in sight, and she wondered if he was deliberately staying out of her way.

Probably worried she'd throw herself at him again.

From the sounds coming down the hallway, she figured he was in the kitchen now. Well, the noise, plus the smell of bacon cooking. Yeah, nothing was getting by her this morning.

She took a deep breath, placing her hand against her stomach in a pathetic attempt to quell the butterflies. Okay, she could do this.

She reached out to turn the knob, then stopped and stepped back. No, she couldn't. She was a coward. God, how could she face him after what she did last night? It didn't matter that he had participated. Well, at least a little. Even though she knew he was fighting it.

Or maybe he had been trying to fend her off.

And really, what was that one kiss all about, anyway? When he had bent over and kissed the top of head like she was some little kid? Or, worse, a puppy dog.

And enough already. She couldn't put this off forever. With a steadying breath, she tossed the backpack over her shoulder and pulled open the door, holding her head high and pretending that she hadn't made the worst sort of fool out of herself the night before.

The smell of bacon was richer as she approached the kitchen and she was surprised when her stomach growled in response. Well, it was nice to know that embarrassment hadn't killed her hunger, at least.

Except she really didn't want to spend any more time with Jay than she needed to.

Stop it, she told herself. Just pretend nothing happened. Just act normal.

Only she didn't know what normal was around Jay, because she had always been kind of quiet and shy around him.

Because she had been crushing on him.

And why, oh why, couldn't she have just kept acting like that last night?

She stopped in the dining room, which was just an extension of the hallway with a pass-through window and small counter next to the door leading into the kitchen. Jay's back was to her as he stood in front of the stove, stirring something in a pan. She took a deep breath and forced a smile on her face.

"I'm ready whenever you are."

Had she imagined the slight stiffening of Jay's back? Probably not. She chewed on her lower lip, wondering if she should say anything else, but he spoke first, stopping her.

"You can at least have some breakfast first. I hear your stomach rumbling from here."

Angie slammed her hand against her stomach, hoping to stop it from making any more noise, but it didn't listen to her. Great. Just one more thing to add to her embarrassment.

Jay didn't say anything else, though, just pulled the pan from the stovetop and sat it off to the side. She watched as he grabbed two plates from a cabinet and spooned some scrambled eggs onto each, followed by a generous helping of bacon. He turned with both plates in his hand and walked past her, sitting them on the table before returning to the kitchen.

"Um, anything I can do to help?"

"Just have a seat."

She turned and dropped her backpack on the floor, then lowered herself to the ladder back chair. Jay came back to the table and placed silverware and a napkin next to her, then returned to the kitchen.

She absently unfolded the napkin—a real cloth one, not a paper towel—and stared down at the plate in front of her.

"Would you like coffee or orange juice or anything?"

"Um, coffee please."

"Cream? Sugar? Black? I don't have any artificial stuff, sorry."

"Cream and sugar is fine."

A minute went by before he returned and placed

a cup of coffee in front of her, the rich brew teasing her nose. She grabbed the cup and took a sip, hoping to use the steam as an excuse for her flaming face.

But she shouldn't have worried, because Jay wasn't even looking at her.

She let out a small sigh and grabbed her fork, playing with the eggs before finally taking a bite. She hadn't known what to expect, hadn't given much thought to Jay's cooking abilities—after all, why should she have? But the food was pretty good, for all that it was just scrambled eggs and bacon.

Long minutes went by, filled with an awkward silence as they both ate. Angie watched him from lowered lids, her embarrassment not detracting from her appreciation of the man in front of her. Close-cropped dark blonde hair, cut a little longer on top. Flint gray eyes, completely focused on the plate in front of him. And the rigid set to his shoulders, broadcasting his discomfort loud and clear.

She was trying not to be obvious. For all the attention he was paying her, though, she could have just propped her chin in her hand and stared at him and he wouldn't have noticed.

She finished chewing the last bit of bacon, washing it down with a final swallow of coffee. The silence was unbearable now, oppressive and damning in its weight. Her hands curled into the napkin on her lap as she wondered if she should say something.

"Jay, about last night—"

He jumped from the table so fast that he knocked into the edge of it. Their plates bounced against the wood surface, the clanging loud in the following silence. But he didn't say anything, just grabbed the empty plates and cups from the table and made a hasty retreat into the kitchen.

Which made her feel even worse. She didn't want this tension between them, this awkwardness that stretched her nerves to an uncomfortable point. Angie lowered her head and stared at her hands, still clutching the twisted napkin.

"I just wanted to—"

Plates banged together with a loud noise, interrupting her. Angie turned and watched as Jay placed everything into the dishwasher, his movements short and jerky. She took a deep breath and let it out, frustration now warring with embarrassment. Didn't he realize she was trying to apologize?

No, he probably thought she was going to proposition him or something.

"Jay, I didn't mean—"

"Angie, stop." Jay slammed the dishwasher closed and finally turned to face her, his eyes boring into hers. The intensity in the gray depths made her heart skip a beat. Had she always known how intensely gorgeous those gray eyes of his were? Or was she just seeing him a different light now?

Probably both.

And she really needed to push all thoughts like that from her mind, because that way lay insanity.

"I just wanted to apologize—"

"Angie, as far as I'm concerned, I'd prefer to completely forget about last night. It didn't happen. It shouldn't have happened. As far as I'm concerned, *nothing* happened. Okay?"

Angie's mouth snapped closed and she looked away, her face flaming under his scrutiny. She heard him mutter something but she refused to look at him.

And she actually thought earlier she couldn't

possibly be more mortified. That's what she got for trying to be optimistic.

She got up from the table then picked up her backpack and slung it over her shoulder, making sure she kept her gaze lowered. It was bad enough that her cheeks were flaming, that he could see the embarrassment so clearly on her face. But to also know that her actions last night had embarrassed him was the last straw. Yeah, she had made a complete ass of herself, but she could have sworn that there had been at least a little mutual attraction and interest coming from him.

Obviously there wasn't, which only made the whole debacle that much worse.

"Got it. So, ready whenever you are."

"Shit." The word was short, conveying the frustration he obviously felt, which only increased her own misery.

She hiked the strap higher on her shoulder and moved closer to the door, figuring she'd just wait for him outside. A strong hand wrapped around her arm, stopping her. She looked down at the hand, momentarily caught off-guard, then raised her eyes to find Jay watching her, something unreadable in the depths of his gaze.

He quickly released her arm and ran his hand down his face with a loud sigh. "Ang, I didn't mean that the way you took it, okay? Listen, last night." He paused and took a deep breath. "You have no idea how flattered—"

"Oh God, stop. Can this get any worse?"

"Ang, let me finish. I don't think you realize how hard it was for me to stop and, well, just to stop. But you're Dave's sister and I can't take advantage of you that way. I *won't* take advantage of you that way. Does that make any sense?"

Angie watched him struggle to explain. No, it didn't make sense. Was he trying to saying he liked her but wouldn't do anything because Dave was her brother? Or was he trying to tell her he thought she was nothing more than a kid?

A flare of frustration shot through her and she tightened her grip on the strap again. "I'm not some innocent kid, Jay. I haven't been for a really long time, so you can stop treating me like one."

"No, you're definitely not a kid." His eyes moved from her face and drifted down her body, and she wondered what he saw underneath the shapeless navy blue scrubs she wore. Was that a flush creeping across his cheeks, or just wishful thinking on her part?

His eyes came back to hers as he took a deep breath and shook his head. "Shit. Yeah, you're definitely not a kid. But you *are* Dave's sister."

The room fell silent, stressing the point Jay was trying to make as strongly as his words. And she understood. Well, maybe a small part of her understood. But there was nothing she could say about it, nothing she could do about it, especially not right now. So Angie just nodded and took a step back, desperate to put more space between them.

"Got it. So, whenever you're ready."

Jay watched her for a few seconds then let out a sigh. He nodded and grabbed his keys from the counter of the pass-through then headed to the door. Angie followed, trying to push all thoughts of Jay from her mind, trying to forget about last night, trying to stomp down the embarrassment that still fanned her cheeks.

All of which would have been a lot easier to do if her eyes weren't so focused on his firm ass as he walked in front of her.

Chapter Four

"Angie told me what you did the other night."

Jay choked on the coffee he had been drinking, the hot liquid going down the wrong way. He sat the cup down, splashing some on the table as he bent over, coughing.

What the fuck?

"What the hell, Jay?"

He coughed some more, a spasm tearing his stomach hard enough he thought he might hurl, then looked over at Mikey Donaldson as she wiped at the coffee splashed on her arm. She turned and fixed him with a questioning look but he only shook his head. He closed his eyes, coughing once more, then turned to look at Dave.

He expected his face to make contact with Dave's fist, and actually flinched when Dave reached out. Only it wasn't with his fist, and certainly not to his face. Instead, the burly paramedic clapped him on the shoulder and smiled.

What the fuck?

"Uh." Jay stopped and cleared his still-burning throat, not sure what to say.

"About her car, how it wouldn't start so you fixed it for her. Thanks for looking out for her."

"Oh, yeah. No problem."

Dave clapped him on the shoulder again then walked over to the counter at the back of the room and fixed himself a cup of coffee. Jay watched as he took a long swallow then leaned against the counter, the mug held loosely in one hand as he watched Jay.

And Jay waited, wondering what else was coming, wondering how he could even begin to defend himself. The fact of the matter was, he couldn't. There was no excuse for letting himself get out of control like he had, and he'd been beating himself up for it for the last few days.

"I honestly have no idea what to do with that girl." Dave shook his head and took another swallow of coffee, a frown on his face.

"Girl? Who are we talking about here?" Mike asked, looking first at Dave, then at Jay, then back to Dave.

"My sister. Angie."

Mike laughed, the sound grating on Jay. He wanted to kick her under the table but was afraid to move because he was still waiting for Dave lay into him.

"Dave, your sister is not a girl. Maybe if you stopped treating her like one, you wouldn't have so many problems."

"Mike, she's my baby sister. She *is* a girl. I just wish she'd get her act together."

Jay opened his mouth, then snapped it shut when he realized he had been ready to jump in and defend

Angie. But he realized that might look suspicious so he said nothing.

"Are we talking about the same sister here? The one who bartends at Duffy's?" Mike tossed the question to Dave as she pushed away from the table. She glanced at Jay, giving him another curious look, then walked over to the sink and grabbed a sponge.

"Yeah, that's her."

"The one who's also going to vet school? The one you bragged about graduating college with top honors? That sister?"

"I only have the one sister and you know it. What's your point, Mike?"

"No point. Just wondering why you think she needs to get her act together, that's all." Mike sponged down the table, grimacing at the spilled coffee, then walked back to the sink to rinse the sponge out.

Just one more thing for Jay to feel guilty about, he realized. He was the one who made the mess, he should've been the one to clean it up. But that paled in comparison to everything else he had to feel guilty about so he didn't let it bother him. Much.

"Because she does. I'm worried about her dating. Her choice in men leaves a lot to be desired and she just needs to get her head on straight."

The urge to bolt from the room was nearly overwhelming and Jay struggled to remain completely still. He could feel a flush starting at the back of his neck and only hoped that neither Dave nor Mike would notice, because he had no idea how he'd explain it. So he just sat there, staring at a spot on the wall behind Dave, and hoped to hell that nobody noticed, that nobody would say anything.

The clanging of a bell broke the silence and all

three of them paused, heads tilted to listen as the radio came to life. Dave muttered something and sat his mug down then left the kitchen to respond to the medic call.

Jay let out a deep breath and turned his attention back to the paper, thankful that Dave didn't seem to have any idea what had really happened the other night.

The paper was suddenly pulled from his hands and he looked up in surprise to see Mikey sitting across from him, her eyebrows raised in question.

"Anything you want to tell me?"

"What? No. Why?" Jay raised the paper again, making sure it covered his heated face. He should have known that wouldn't work, though, because Mike's hand wrapped around the top edge and pulled it back down. Only this time, she kept her hand on it, holding it flat against the table.

"You want to maybe rethink that?"

"I have no idea what you're talking about."

"Really?" Mike pulled the paper toward her and carefully folded it, her eyes never leaving his face. He took a deep breath and forced his eyes to meet hers. Why, he didn't know. She obviously already knew something was going on.

A few long seconds went by, filled with Mike's questioning look and his squirming. He finally gave up and looked away.

"It's not what you're thinking so stop looking at me that way."

"Then what is it?"

Jay pursed his lips, wondering how much to tell her. Mikey was his best friend, and there had never really been any secrets between them. But for some reason, he just couldn't seem to tell her what happened. At least, not everything. So he decided on an abbreviated—and definitely G-rated—version.

"Her car broke down the other night after work, and she needed a new alternator. So, I fixed it for her. End of story."

Another minute went by while Mike just studied him, saying nothing. Jay started to squirm under her steady gaze and had to force himself to stop before it made him look guiltier than he actually was.

"So you fixed her alternator? That's it?"

"Well no, she needed a new one."

"Oh. And you just happened to have on laying around at, what, two o'clock in the morning outside Duffy's?"

"Of course not, no. I bought a new one for her the next day and replaced it."

"Hm." She sat back in the chair and just watched him, her fingers tapping on the table in front of her. Once again, Jay was forced to squelch his desire to squirm.

And he still couldn't quite meet her eyes.

"Why do I get the impression that there's a lot more you're not telling me?"

"I have no idea what you're talking about."

"Really?" Another few seconds went by, and Jay thought that maybe she'd stop asking questions. But no, that would have been too much to expect. "Jay, did you sleep with Angie?"

"What?" Jay nearly jumped from the chair, then caught himself at the last minute. "No, of course not. Do you really think that I'd—"

"Then what happened?"

"I told you."

"Yeah, and again, you're leaving something out. Now out with it."

Jay opened his mouth to reply without really knowing what he was going to say. But he was stopped from saying anything when the alarm went off, literally saved by the bell. He muttered a small prayer of thanks and started heading out to the engine, Mike right beside him.

"I'm not letting you off the hook, Jay."

He said nothing, just quickly dressed in his turnout gear then ran for the engine. Of course Mikey wouldn't let it go. That would be too much to expect.

Chapter Five

Duffy's was crowded. Again.

Angie didn't know why she was surprised, or even why she was complaining. The weekend business had been steadily increasing over the last year, which is why she even had this job. The pay was good, the tips great, and she had flexible work-hours scheduled around school and her internship.

And she really did enjoy working here. Tonight's crowd was already off to a generous start, which was normal for second Saturday thanks to the live band that was now regularly scheduled. So really, Angie shouldn't be complaining at all.

And she wasn't, not really. In fact, tonight shouldn't be any different than any other night she worked here.

Except her brother was here with all of his coworkers.

Including Jay.

Tonight was the first time that she had seen Jay since last week, and the memory of that whole catastrophe still brought a flush to her face. So yeah, she should have been happy that he barely acknowledged her when he walked in. She should be happy that he wasn't paying any attention to her at all as he laughed and joked with his friends in the back corner.

Yeah, that's what she kept trying to tell herself.

Angie reached into the cooler and grabbed four bottles, grateful for the momentary coolness that brushed her skin. She sat all four bottles on the bar and pulled the bottle opener from her back pocket, then quickly popped the tops on each. She reached behind her and grabbed two glasses and filled them with ice, then poured tea into them from the pitcher next to her.

She made a quick note on the sales slip then turned and placed the glasses on the tray next to the bottles. "There you go."

Michaela Donaldson—Mike to her coworkers, which included both Dave and Jay—gave her a smile and tossed a bill on the bar next to the drinks. Angie nodded her thanks and tossed the ten into the tip jar, surprised that the woman made no move to take the drinks.

But not surprised that it was anyone but Jay who had come up to get the drinks. In fact, Jay hadn't even come close to the bar since walking in.

So what did that tell her?

Way too much.

Angie looked back at Mike, wondering if maybe she had forgotten a drink because she didn't understand why she would still be standing there, watching her. Especially since the band was on break. Mike's boyfriend, Nick, was the band's lead singer and guitarist and the woman generally spent the breaks with him. But Mike just stood there watching her, saying nothing. Angie couldn't waste any more time worrying about it because there was a line of people still waiting to be served.

Breaks were always hectic. Business was steady throughout the night, but she and Rick had to really hustle to keep up during breaks. And right now it was just her, because Rick had to run to the back to grab more cases for the cooler.

So Angie ignored the woman watching her and waited on the next two customers, pouring drinks and taking money and moving on to the next two. She felt Rick push behind her and she stepped closer to the bar, moving out of his way so he could put the beer into the cooler.

"He can be an ass sometimes, so don't let him get to you."

Angie looked over in surprise, noticing that Mike was still standing there, now balancing the tray full of drinks in her hands. The woman gave her a friendly smile then turned away, disappearing into the crowd before Angie could say anything.

What had that been about? She couldn't have been talking about Rick. So did that mean she was talking about Jay? Who else would she mean? But why would she even say anything at all? Unless Jay had said something—and she didn't even want to think about that possibility. It was entirely too embarrassing.

Angie shook her head, refusing to think about it as she turned her attention to the next two customers. She had to keep focused and think about her job here tonight, not waste valuable time worrying about something that probably meant nothing.

But the thought was there, waiting for her as she went through the motions for the next hour, fighting for attention she couldn't spare. And the more she tried to push it away, the harder it fought to be given center stage. The frustration built inside her until she finally snapped and balled up the wet dishrag and threw it into the sink with a small curse.

"You okay?" The question came from Rick and she looked over, noticed him watching her in curiosity. She blew out a deep breath and pushed the hair out of her face.

"Yeah, I'm fine."

"You look frustrated. Why don't you go outside for a quick break? I can handle it for a few."

A break suddenly sounded like a perfect idea so she nodded her thanks and made her way to the service door at the back of the bar. The door closed behind her, immediately muting the noise of the crowd. Angie took a deep breath and kept walking, finally pushing open the outside door and stepping into the night air.

The noise from inside was noticeably less now, the air cooler than the stuffiness of so many bodies inside. She took another deep breath then lowered herself to the bench pushed against the wall and closed her eyes.

Rick was right, this was just the break she needed. No noise, no crowds, nobody clamoring for attention. Yeah, she normally loved this job. But tonight, for some reason, things just weren't clicking.

For some reason? Angie laughed to herself. She knew exactly why, and she needed to just get over it.

She reached behind her and grabbed the length

of her hair, twisting it then pulling it off her neck, wishing briefly she could just pull it back in a ponytail. That's how she generally wore her hair, anyway. But not here. For some reason, she always wore it down while she was bartending.

Which was just one more thing she could add to the list of things she did that made no sense. Like throw herself at guys who had absolutely no interest in her.

She waited a few more minutes, letting her body relax in the quiet of the night, then made her way back inside. Rick looked over at her and she gave him a thumbs-up, nodding her head in thanks for the break, then turned to the crowd at the bar.

And immediately wished she hadn't.

Jay was leaning against the counter, his left arm resting against the varnished top as he chewed on a stir stick and watched her. Angie's breath hitched in her chest as those gray eyes studied her, and she suddenly wished that she could call Rick over to take her place.

But she couldn't, because Rick was handling other customers. So Angie stood a little straighter and forced a smile on her face then closed the distance between her and Jay, hoping she at least looked calm on the outside.

Her eyes briefly met his before she dropped her gaze, unable to focus under the watchfulness of those mesmerizing gray eyes. Now her eyes rested on his throat, dropping lower to the open collar of his linen shirt, unbuttoned just enough to expose the tanned skin of his broad chest.

She swallowed and looked away, hoping she hadn't just been caught staring. "Another round?" She didn't bother looking back at him, just moved to the side to reach the cooler so she could grab the beer. His hand closed over her arm, stopping her. She tried to ignore the excitement his touch caused, the involuntary shiver that radiated through her arm to her chest, making her heart beat a little harder.

She knew she should shake off his hand but she couldn't, not when the warmth of his palm against her flesh held her imprisoned, as much as the steady gaze of his eyes held her immobile.

He watched her for a few seconds that seemed so much longer, time slowing around them, his presence and steady gaze pushing everyone around them from her mind. Angie swallowed, not sure what to say, then lowered her eyes to where his hand still rested on her arm, branding her.

"No, don't worry about another round. I just want..." His voice drifted off and Angie held her breath, watching, waiting. Jay looked down at his hand then quickly pulled it away, breaking the contact as if he had just realized he was touching her. He cleared his throat then pulled the stirrer from his mouth, no longer looking at her.

"Uh, I'll just have one this time."

Angie nodded, swallowing her disappointment, then reached down and pulled a bottle from the cooler. She popped the top, slid it toward him, turned to leave.

"You okay?"

She paused, half-tempted to just ignore him, then shook her head with a weary sigh. She turned back, not quite facing him, and busied herself with straightening the stack of coasters at the edge of the bar.

"Yup, I'm fine." Angie looked up at him, then quickly away. "And thanks. For fixing my car, I mean. You didn't have to do that."

Jay brought the bottle to his lips and took a long swallow, his eyes never leaving hers. She watched his strong throat work and felt butterflies take wing in her stomach. "No problem."

"You'll have to let me know how much I owe you."

"My treat."

"Jay, I can't let you do that. I know it wasn't cheap."

"I said, no problem. I told you I'd look out for you."

Angie clenched her jaw, knowing he had said no such thing, and knowing that the comment was supposed to remind her that he thought she was a kid. That she was someone who needed looking after. She glanced around to make sure there were no waiting customers, then leaned forward. "No, you didn't. And I told you already, I'm not some kid who needs watching after. Let me know how much I owe you."

Jay watched her for a long minute, the expression in his eyes unreadable. Angie straightened, suddenly needing to put more distance between them. She was ready to turn and walk away, to start the nightly process of cleaning up, when his next words stopped her.

"Fine. Have dinner with me next week."

"Uh—"

"I'll let you know when." He looked at her for another second then turned and walked away, disappearing into the crowd.

Angie was frozen in place, wondering if she had heard correctly. Had Jay just asked her out on a date? No, surely she had heard wrong. Or she was reading too much into it. Why would he have asked her out, after letting her know, repeatedly, that he only saw her as Dave's kid sister? It didn't make sense.

A customer stepped into her line of vision, pulling her from the confusing tumble of thoughts threatening to drown her. So she forced a smile on her face and greeted the customer, telling herself it was time to get back to work.

Chapter Six

"On my count."

"All set?"

"I'm right behind you, Jay."

"And three."

Jay grunted as he lifted the bottom rail of the chair, feeling the brunt of three hundred pounds of humanity bear straight down into his arms. He stepped back with his left foot, feeling air beneath it before it finding the next stair. Mike had a tight grip on the back of his pants, leading him down each step, guiding him by word and touch, one by one.

Above him, he could hear labored breathing: the heavy wet sound of the patient's gasping, the steady breathing of Dave's exertion as they made the descent step by agonizing step.

Dammit, why were the heavy ones always on the top floor?

They reached the landing and righted the chair, quickly transferring the patient to the stretcher then wheeling him to the medic unit. Jay jumped in behind

Dave, helping him get the monitor back in place while Jimmy Hughes, Dave's partner, switched the patient to the onboard oxygen.

"Need anything else?" Jay asked as he stepped out of the medic.

"Nope, we're good. Save us some lunch." Dave grinned then motioned for Jimmy to get going. Jay slammed the back doors shut and watched as the medic pulled away. He groaned and stretched his back, then wrapped his arms around himself to stretch his shoulders.

"What's the matter, Jay? Getting old?" Mike nudged him as they walked back to the engine and he shot her a dirty look.

"Ha ha, very funny. You can carry him down next time." This was the third time this month they had been called to the patient's apartment, and Jay had drawn short straw all three times when it came time to carry him down the stairs. He didn't want to think how much worse it would be in a few weeks, when summer finally arrived.

"Nope. You lost, fair and square. Deal with it."

Jay ignored her and climbed into the engine, propping his foot on the seat in front of him and strapping himself in before the engine took off. He closed his eyes and leaned his head back in the seat, wishing the roar of the engine was loud enough to drown out his thoughts.

Tonight was the night he was supposed to meet Angie for dinner, and he still had no idea what he was going to do about it. Hell, he still didn't know what had possessed him to even bring it up. To ask her out. And he hadn't even really asked her—he'd pretty much just told her. It had not been one of his finest moments.

But he had been watching her all night last Saturday, trying not to be obvious because he didn't want Dave to catch him. Christ, he could just imagine what would happen then. She had looked frazzled for a good part of the evening, and he hoped it hadn't been because of him.

And every damn time he tried to come up with a way to distract himself, something else happened and he found himself looking back at the bar, his eyes automatically finding Angie. Watching her.

It was like he was suddenly obsessed and couldn't get her off his mind, and he had no idea why. Couldn't stop thinking about her. In fact, he hadn't been able to stop thinking of her since the morning he dropped her off at the vet clinic.

The morning after his truly shining moment, when he had damn near slept with her. When he had damn near fucked his friend's little sister.

To make matters worse, he was pretty sure Mike had caught him watching Angie and figured out something was going on, if the look she had given him was any indication. That was when he had finally gone to the bar, just to get away from Mike. Yeah, sure it was. Then Angie had made that stupid comment, saying she'd pay him back for the alternator. Yeah, something had short-circuited in his brain.

So tonight, he was meeting Angie for dinner.

Jay rubbed his hands over his face and looked over at Mike, wondering if maybe he should talk to her about all of this. Surely she'd have some advice for him.

Or maybe knock some sense into him.

Which was exactly what he needed, because he still couldn't believe he was meeting his friend's sister. For a date.

No. It was not a date. It was just dinner. So she wouldn't feel the need to pay him back.

Yeah, he just needed to keep telling himself that. Maybe he'd finally believe it by the time tonight rolled around.

His radio squealed and he leaned down to turn it up at the same time Pete turned around in the seat up front and banged on the cab window. He raised his index finger, holding it up and twirling it in a circle.

Jay unbuckled his harness and grabbed his gear, jumping into the turnout pants as the engine's siren began its long wail. He shrugged into the coat and quickly snapped it closed then sat back down, pulling the straps of the breathing apparatus over his shoulders and fastening them. Mike banged on the engine hood to get his attention, giving him the thumbs-up when he looked at her.

Perfect. They were headed to a working fire, which was the next best thing to getting his mind off the situation he had gotten himself mixed up in.

The best thing would be if he didn't have to show up at all.

**

Angie glanced at her watch for the tenth time in as many minutes and tried convincing herself that she really wasn't a fool. Her argument fell flat, though, because only a fool would wait more than an hour before admitting they had been stood up.

So yeah, as painful as it was, Angie had to admit she was a fool, because it was past seven o'clock and there was still no sign of Jay.

And she was still waiting.

She propped her chin in one hand and idly drew circles in the puddle of condensation left by her drink. A flare of painful disappointment shot through her chest and she ruthlessly pushed it away, thinking that it wasn't worth wasting the time, effort, or even energy in being disappointed.

No, it was better to be thankful that she had decided to sit at the bar instead of getting a table, because wouldn't that have been an even more pathetic picture? She shook her head and admonished herself for entertaining the idea that this was going to be an actual date.

It was a little tough having a date by yourself.

Angie signaled the bartender and asked for her check, then handed him her credit card as soon as he brought it over. Now that she had decided to finally leave, something she should have done an hour ago, she didn't want to wait a minute longer than she had to.

And she had no one else to blame but herself for her foolishness. From embarrassing herself by throwing herself at Jay that night at his apartment, to getting excited when he suggested they meet for dinner, to waiting entirely too long for him to show up. It was her own fault, all of it. And it was no more than she deserved for spinning some stupid fantasy around a silly crush. No wonder all of Dave's friends thought of her as some kid—she had been acting as silly as some love-struck teenaged girl.

The bartender came back with her receipt and she quickly signed her name, leaving a generous tip before sliding the receipt to the edge of the bar. She finished the last of her drink, grabbed her bag from the back of the stool, then stood up.

It was time to push all thoughts of Jay from her mind. She had studying to do and work to finish, things she had let fall behind because of some stupid adolescent crush on her brother's friend. Well, no more.

She pushed through the door of the restaurant and into the warm evening air, ignoring the patrons that were still waiting on tables to open up. She turned down the sidewalk and crossed into the parking lot, already making a mental list of things she had to do, when she heard someone call her name. Her steps faltered and she looked around, wondering who would be calling her when a car horn blared behind her, followed by the squeal of rubber against asphalt.

A force knocked into her, pushing her out of the way and startling her more than the car she had inadvertently walked in front of. Her pulse rate jumped frantically as the car went by, the driver shouting an obscenity at her. Angie ignored it, more concerned about the solid body so close to hers. She reached up and pushed against the chest that was mere inches from her nose, trying to escape her would-be rescuer.

"Holy shit, Ang. Did you not see that car? You almost got hit!"

Angie stopped struggling and looked up as her mind slowly started registering what happened.

Someone had called her name, distracting her, and she had nearly stepped into the path of an oncoming car.

Only to be rescued by the same person who had

distracted her in the first place.

Jay.

She pushed away from him with enough force to break the hold of his arms around her and stepped back, surprised at the look of concern on his face. Instead of reassuring her, his expression fueled her sudden anger. If he hadn't called out to her, if he had bothered showing up on time, she wouldn't have nearly walked in front of the car.

Which meant everything was his fault.

She pushed the hair from her face and stared at Jay, her jaw clenched and her mouth pursed in a straight line as she fought with herself to keep her temper. She wanted to rail at him, to yell and let him know exactly what she thought.

But her insides were still shaking, her hands still trembling from the close call, and she couldn't get the words to make the journey from her mind to her mouth. So she said nothing, just turned away from him and continued walking to her car, determined to ignore him.

He caught up with her, stopping her with a hand on her shoulder.

"Angie, are you okay? What's wrong?"

"Wrong? Nothing is wrong. Good night." She brushed his hand from her shoulder and kept walking, wishing she could be wittier and let him know exactly what she thought. It would have been even better if she had just kept her mouth shut because her stupid voice sounded a little shaky. At least to her. Maybe Jay didn't notice.

She reached her car and leaned down to unlock it so she could open the door, wanting nothing more than to go home and put this disastrous night behind her. But Jay was beside her once again, his body between her and escape.

"I'm sorry I'm late. We had a fire and didn't get relieved until late and I was going to call except I don't have your number." His explanation was rushed, as if he realized that she wasn't interested in hearing it, that she wasn't going to give him time to explain.

And he would be right, because she *wasn't* interested. It didn't matter, because she had already realized she was a fool for thinking anything could come of her stupid crush and she was now over it. So she looked up at him and gave him a small smile and nodded.

"You don't have my number? That's funny, because I could have sworn that you called Dave the other day. But hey, no problem. Now if you'll excuse me, I have things I need to do." She tried pushing him away so she could open the door but he still wouldn't budge. She stepped back and fixed him with what she hoped was an intimidating stare. The move backfired, because he was giving her his own intimidating stare, one definitely more effective than hers.

"I meant I didn't have your cell number, and I couldn't call the house."

"Really Jay? And why's that?"

"You know why."

"No, I don't. Why don't you explain it to me?" She knew what he would say, of course. He couldn't call the house because Dave might answer the phone. And God forbid if he let her brother know that he planned on meeting her.

Jay didn't answer, just looked down at her with

those eyes she found so mesmerizing. And he still didn't move, the seconds stretching around them as his warm gaze searched her face. A small smile suddenly tilted up the corner of his mouth. "At least let me buy you a drink to make up for being an ass."

The man infuriated her. He thought he could just smile and offer to buy her a drink and that would be that? Well, why wouldn't he think that, after she had all but thrown herself at him? And the worst part was that she was tempted to say yes.

Which infuriated her even more.

So she clenched her jaw and pushed against him one more time, grateful that he actually stepped back. She tossed him a look then opened her car door and slid into the seat.

"Not interested, but thanks anyway." She ignored the look of surprise on his face as she jammed the key into the ignition and closed the door. She threw the car into reverse and backed out of the parking space, only partly disappointed to see that Jay had taken a step back, because she would've taken perverse pleasure in running over his foot.

She straightened the wheel, jammed the car into drive, and wasted no time in pulling away. A horn blared from behind her but she paid no attention, only wanting to put distance between her and the man watching her before she changed her mind and did something stupid.

Like take him up on his offer of having a drink.

But that didn't stop her from watching his figure in the rearview mirror, and imagining that she saw a look of disappointment etched into his face as she drove away.

Chapter Seven

"You're awfully quiet tonight."

Angie looked over at her brother, noticing the frown on his face as he leaned against the door frame separating the living room from the dining room and watched her. She offered him a shrug and turned back to the television set, pretending to be engrossed in the drama playing across the large screen.

"Just tired, I guess."

"You're working too much. You're going to burn yourself out if you're not careful." He walked over to the sofa and pushed her feet off to the side then took a seat, which forced her to shift positions. She shot him a dirty look then pushed herself to a sitting position, curling her legs under her.

"Is there a reason you have to sit there, when the love seat is completely empty?"

He gave her a surprised look, the slash of one brow raising in question. "I like this spot."

She shook her head but said nothing, just tried to let her attention go back to the movie. It didn't work.

Of course, she hadn't really been paying attention to begin with.

"So did you hear what I said?"

"About what?"

"About you burning yourself out. You're working too much."

"No, I'm not. And I'm not burning myself out."

"Yeah, well, I think you should think about cutting down your hours at the bar. Better yet, you should just quit."

Angie let out a heavy sigh, putting more emphasis on it than she should. They had already had this conversation. Repeatedly. And she didn't feel like getting into it again.

She grabbed the remote and turned up the volume, hoping Dave would take the hint. Instead, he took the remote from her hand and put the television on mute. "I'm being serious, Angela."

She grimaced at the use of her full name and turned to face him. There was no use in even trying to pretend to watch television now, even if she had been interested in the program.

"You don't have a say in what I do, *David*. That control freak stuff might work at work, but not here."

"Control freak?"

"Yeah, control freak. All your ex-military, Mr. Medic control stuff."

"Angela, we're not talking about me, we're talking about you and I'm telling you, you need to think about what you're doing."

"No, we're not talking about me, because I'm not putting up with this anymore." She pushed herself off the sofa and jammed her feet into her slippers.

"Where are you going?"

"To my room. Away from you. Alone."

"Angie, wait."

She turned and looked down at him, feeling some of her ire disappear at the look of concern etched deep into his face. How could she be irritated, when she knew he was only trying to watch out for her? She sighed and sat back down. "Dave, you have to stop treating me like a little kid."

He sat back as if she had slapped him. His brows lowered in a frown and small creases showed at the corners of his eyes, making him suddenly look older than his thirty-two years. The fight left her as quickly as it appeared. He had been distracted lately, worn-out and tired. And he really was only looking out for her, even if he didn't realize she didn't need it.

"You're my kid sister, Angie. I'm always going to worry about you."

"There's a difference between worrying, and treating me like I don't know what I'm doing. And you've been doing that for two years, ever since you got back. You have to stop, Dave. I know how to take care of myself."

He watched her for a long minute, his dark eyes boring into her, like he was trying to figure out a puzzle, before he finally looked away and sighed. "Listen, I know you can take care of yourself. I just don't understand why you feel the need to wear yourself out between the internship and school and the bar. You need to slow down, do something for fun."

Angie almost laughed. If he only knew. But she didn't think he'd find any humor in the things that she'd done the past several weeks, so she said nothing and hoped that maybe he would understand what she was trying to say. "Dave, I do make time for fun. And I enjoy working at the bar. It's an escape for me."

"Will you just think about cutting back your hours?"

Angie sighed. So much for trying to get him to understand. "No, Dave, I won't. Not unless it really becomes an issue, which it won't."

A flash of irritation flared in his dark eyes and she braced herself for another lecture. But he surprised her by merely shaking his head. "We can talk about this later. At least remember to take off for the camping trip. It's coming up, the end of June. Plenty of time for you to ask off."

A feeling close to panic rushed through her at the reminder. She had completely forgotten about the annual family camping trip that Dave and his shift went on each summer in West Virginia. It was a completely rustic experience, with everyone sleeping in tents and cooking over an open campfire. The four days were filled with stories and hiking and even rafting or kayaking along the river. She had gone the last two years and surprised herself by having so much fun in what was essentially the middle of nowhere.

The thought of going now didn't fill her with fun. No, it filled her with panic.

Because Jay would be there.

And she didn't think she could handle being stuck in the middle of nowhere for four days with Jay, no matter how many other people would be there. She opened her mouth, not sure what excuse she would give Dave to get out of going, but was stopped from saying anything when the phone rang.

Dave looked at her strangely and she had the

funny feeling that he knew she was going to try to get out of it. He didn't say anything, though, just leaned over and grabbed the phone, answering it with his usual gruff, "Yeah?"

Angie closed her eyes, thankful for the distraction, no matter how short-lived it would be. But even a momentary distraction was better than nothing, because it gave her a chance to come up with a better excuse for not going.

"Hey Jay, what's up?"

Angie's eyes shot open at Dave's greeting and she silently berated herself for letting her heart race at the sound of Jay's name. Telling herself once again that she was a fool, she stood up from the sofa, ready to head to her room and just call it a night. Her foot was on the bottom step when Dave's next words stopped her.

"Angie? Yeah, she's here." Dave paused, turning to give her an odd look. "You want to talk to Angie? My sister? Yeah, okay, hang on."

Dave held the phone out to her, his gaze direct and curious. Angie stared at him, then looked down at the phone in his outstretched hand. She had the sudden impulse to run straight upstairs and lock herself in her room but stopped herself from giving into it. Barely.

"It's Jay. He wants to talk to you." Dave stood up and walked toward her, holding the phone out to her with a look that clearly expressed his confusion.

She was sure she had a similar expression on her face as she slowly reached for the phone. Dave continued to watch her as she took it and held it to her ear.

"Hello?" Did she imagine it, or had her voice

shook ever so slightly? And why was Dave watching her so closely?

"Hey. I, uh, I didn't catch you at a bad time, did I?"

"No."

"Okay, good. That's good." There was a pause on the other end and Angie waited, not sure if he expected her to say anything. "Listen, about tonight. I just wanted to tell you again I was sorry."

"Oh. Um, okay, sure." Her eyes darted back to Dave and she squirmed under his scrutiny.

"I know you're probably going to say no and I can't blame you, but I really would like to make it up to you. Maybe Friday night, if you're not working? I'm off, so I won't run late this time."

"Um, I'm not sure." Angie gave her brother a dirty look then turned away, heading into the dining room for some privacy.

There was a short laugh from the other end of the phone, and she couldn't tell if it was supposed to a funny laugh, or a sarcastic laugh.

"You're not sure you're working? Or you're not sure you want to go?"

"I'm not working, no."

There was another pause, broken by a soft sigh. "So does that mean you want to meet?"

"I'm not really sure." Angie looked over her shoulder, not surprised to see that Dave had moved from the living room and was now standing behind her. Not so close that he was breathing down her neck, but close enough to make her acutely aware that he was listening to every word. She gave him a look meant to tell him to mind his own business, which he, of course, completely ignored.

"Could you help me out here, Ang? I don't understand exactly what you're saying. Did you want to meet, or not?" There was another pause, but before she could say anything, she heard something that sounded suspiciously like muttered swearing coming from the other end. "Dave's right there, isn't he? Dammit, I knew it was a bad idea to call you at home. Listen, just tell him I'm checking up on how the alternator is working or something."

"Really? Like that will work? Yeah, the alternator's fine, thanks." She didn't try to keep the disbelief from her voice. Did he really think Dave would buy that? So okay, her brother actually stepped back and moved a few feet away from her, a look of something that almost resembled relief crossing his face. But she wasn't naïve enough to think he wasn't going to question her about the call.

"So about Friday night. Yes, or no?"

Angie clenched her jaw, not sure if she should be insulted at the way he was asking her out—if that's what he was really doing. He was probably asking out of guilt or pity, or a combination of both. And she planned on telling him no, she wasn't interested. Right up until she opened her mouth. "Yeah, sure."

"Great. I'm looking forward to it. Listen, I'll call you tomorrow night from work, since I know Dave won't be there. Are you going to be home?"

"Yup, all night." She knew she sounded less than enthusiastic, and figured Jay had to pick up on it. But if he did, he didn't let on because he just chuckled, the sound deep and warm in her ear.

"Great, I'll talk to you tomorrow night." And he hung up before she could respond, before she could tell him that no, she changed her mind, she didn't want to go out Friday night.

She lowered the phone and stared at it for a few seconds, then walked back to place it in the charger. Dave watched her the entire time but didn't say anything, and she actually thought she was going to get away without answering any questions.

Right up until she turned to head upstairs to her room.

"So. Jay called you." Angie turned and looked at him, not trying to hide her annoyance. "What did he want?"

"He was just asking about my car."

"Hm." Dave watched her, his dark eyes serious as they studied her face, and she had to force herself not to squirm under his scrutiny. "It didn't sound like you were just talking about your car."

"Really Dave? Why the third degree? What else would we be talking about?"

"I don't know, that's why I'm asking."

"Nothing, Dave. We were talking about nothing, okay? I'm going to bed." Angie turned and walked away, feeling Dave's stare clear to the base of her spine as she made her way upstairs.

She made it to her room and barely refrained from slamming her door shut. She was upset, but she didn't know what upset her more.

The fact that she couldn't seem to say no to Jay.

The fact that her brother still treated her like a little kid, checking on her every move.

The fact that she realized Jay was right, and knew Dave wouldn't be happy about her seeing him, even if it was just one time.

All three reasons were more than enough to upset her, and she didn't like the feeling.

At all.

Chapter Eight

The sun was just beginning its western descent, dropping low enough that the buildings were finally able to offer some shade. The crowds along the sidewalk were noisy, laughing and joking as they jostled against each other. Jay stepped closer to the building, out of the way, and reached behind him to pull the material of his dress jacket and shirt away from his back. It wasn't especially hot, but between the late evening sun and his unexplained nerves, he wasn't as cool as he'd prefer to be.

And while he didn't want to admit it, he knew his discomfort was mostly from nerves. Just like he didn't want to admit he knew why, but he couldn't lie to himself.

He was nervous about meeting Angie.

Not for the first time, he mentally kicked himself for asking her out. And then he kicked himself for asking her to meet him down here. What the hell kind of date did that? The guy generally picked his date up, didn't ask her to meet him downtown.

Except this wasn't really a date.

Yeah, bullshit.

That's why he was standing here outside a fancy restaurant, dressed to impress in a fucking suit, trying not to fidget.

He could try to spin it any way he liked, but it all came down to whether or not he was going to be honest with himself. So yeah, no matter what story he might tell anyone else, he had to admit to himself that, in his mind at least, this was a date, plain and simple.

What he couldn't understand was why he had asked Angie out tonight. He knew it was wrong, knew it could only lead to trouble. You didn't date your friend's sister, there was a code against that kind of thing. And if you did, you sure as hell didn't do it behind everyone's back.

So why was he doing it?

Jay looked down at the toes of his dress shoes, searching for the answer to that question for the hundredth time today. If he was going to be honest, the answer was: he really didn't know. The only thing he knew was that he couldn't get Angie out of his mind, no matter what he did. He wanted to get to know her better.

And no, it had nothing to do with that night at his house. Yes, he admitted that the memory of her standing in front of him, her body bared for his eyes as she touched herself, had definitely replayed in his mind more than once.

But mostly it was her smile and her laughter that he pictured when he thought of her—which was too frequently, for his peace of mind. He just wanted to get to know her better.

He hadn't wanted to get to know a woman—any woman—like that in entirely too long. That in itself was enough to worry him. Add to that the fact that Angie was Dave's sister and there was a recipe ripe for disaster.

Should it worry him that he wasn't as worried as he should be?

Probably.

But it didn't matter, not right now, because Angie should be here in the next few minutes. He hoped she would be here. Again, he mentally kicked himself for not offering to pick her up. What kind of jackass didn't pick up his date?

The kind of jackass that wouldn't admit that this was an actual date.

He stopped arguing with himself and looked around at the people passing by. It was a Friday night, and the crowd was shifting from businessmen and commuters to people enjoying a night out. His eyes searched the crowds, looking for a single girl standing out among the couples and groups walking by. He didn't see anyone yet but told himself not to worry, that she would show up.

He should have picked her up.

Two taxis pulled up to the curb, and Jay let his gaze drift over to them. A couple got out of the first one. The passenger was still in the second one, the back door open and one shapely leg clad in a high heeled shoe peeking out. Jay let his eyes roam appreciatively over the toned expanse of tan flesh then continued searching the crowd, hoping to see Angie walking toward him.

Still no sign of her. He sighed and glanced at his watch, wondering if maybe she was stuck in traffic or having a hard time finding a place to park. He refused to think she wouldn't show up.

"Hey Jay."

Relief flooded him when he heard his name called and he turned around, a smile on his face. He froze, his mind having trouble processing what his eyes were seeing.

Angie stood a few feet away, at the curb where the taxi he noticed earlier was now pulling away. She was dressed in a simple black dress that fell mid-thigh, cut deep enough to show off lush cleavage. His eyes raked her once more in appreciation, traveling down her tanned legs and stopping at the dangerously high black sandals on her feet.

He swallowed and raised his gaze, noticing the way her dark hair was carelessly pulled up, the length of it off her shoulders with thick strands waving around her face and along her neck. The sun caught it in its dying rays, turning the browns into shades of cinnamon and roan.

And hell, he didn't even know what color roan was.

Her smile faltered and he realized he had been staring like an idiot, frozen at the sight of her. He offered her a smile and closed the distance between them, leaning down and giving her a quick kiss on the cheek before he could stop and think about. The action seemed to surprise her, but she didn't say anything.

"You're beautiful." Jay cursed himself for uttering such a plainly generic phrase, thinking that a woman would want to hear something more poetic or fancier. But he was neither of those things, and the honest declaration was the truth. The compliment seemed to surprise her, though, because a small flush spread across her cheeks and she looked away.

They stood there for a few seconds, neither of them saying anything, and Jay suddenly wondered if Angie was as uncomfortable as he was. If that was the case, they were both going to be in for a long night.

And he didn't want that.

So he reached down and grabbed her hand, threading his fingers through hers and leading her toward the restaurant. "Are you hungry?"

"Yes, actually, I am." Angie said it like it surprised her and he looked over at her, wondering at the comment. But he didn't say anything, just gave her a smile as they stopped at the hostess stand.

They were quickly seated and filled the first few minutes with vague small talk until the waitress came over, took their drink order, then left. Jay looked over at Angie, watching her as she studied the menu.

"Is this okay? I didn't stop to think—"

"No, this is great. Thanks." She looked up and offered him a small smile, then turned back to the menu. "It all looks so good, I just don't know what to get."

"Well, I'll go out on a limb and say that their steak is probably pretty good."

Angie looked up at him, a small frown on her face. Then she finally laughed. Jay let out his breath, glad that she had understood his lame joke. They were at a steak house, a well-known one, so it went without saying that the steak would be good.

The waitress approached with their drinks then took their order. Jay was gratified to hear Angie order the petit filet. He had been on too many dates with too many women who ordered nothing more than a salad, then picked at it all night. It had always made him uncomfortable to eat his own heavy meal, and he invariably left still hungry.

He didn't think he'd have that problem tonight, and ordered the prime rib. The waitress left and he turned back to Angie, raising his beer glass as if he was going to make a toast. She looked at him oddly for a second, then raised her own wine glass in response.

"To the start of a fun date." He had meant to words to be light, but there must have been something in his voice that didn't come out quite right. Angie clinked her glass against his and took a sip of her wine, but instead of smiling like he had hoped, she looked down at the table. Her hand smoothed the white linen of the table cloth then absently straightened the heavy silverware.

He sat back in his chair and watched her, wondering why she suddenly seemed to find the table so much more interesting. "Is everything okay, Angie? Did I say something wrong?"

She looked up at him, a shadow of something uncertain flashing in her dark eyes. She shook her head, paused, then shrugged and took another sip of wine. "No, nothing's wrong. I guess I was just a little confused."

"About what?"

She looked over at him again, her gaze direct and unwavering. "Is that what this really is? A date? Or is it something else?"

Discomfort quickly filled Jay and he glanced away. How was he supposed to answer that, when he had been grappling with the same exact question not even a half hour ago? He knew what he wanted it to be, no matter how much guilt he felt about it. But he didn't know what Angie thought about the whole thing.

She shifted in the chair across from him and he realized he had waited too long to answer her question. That by saying nothing, he had given her the wrong idea, left her with the wrong impression. He opened his mouth, but she started talking before he could.

"Jay, listen, I appreciate it. Really, I do. But you didn't have to do this. I'm a big girl, I don't need you doing—" she paused before waving her hands over the table between them, "whatever this is that you're doing."

"Angie—"

"No, it's okay, really." She gave him a small smile then pushed her chair back from the table, ready to stand up. "Let me see if I can catch the waitress. It's probably not too late to cancel the order and—"

"No." Jay stood up and walked over to her, his hand gently pushing her back into the chair. "Angie, no. I don't want to cancel this. I want to be here tonight, with you, and enjoy our dinner together."

She strained her neck back and stared up at him, looking uncomfortable. He realized that he was now towering over her so he shifted and bent down so they were eye level. Before he could stop himself, he reached out and took her hand, his thumb tracing a circle against her knuckles.

"Listen, I don't know if this is a date or not. I guess that's up to you. What I do know is that I haven't been able to stop thinking about you. I should, but I can't. And I'd like to get to know you better. So maybe this is a date, I don't know. But will you at least have dinner with me, and see how it turns out? You don't have to stay after that if you don't want to. I'll take you to your car and even pay for your parking."

"Jay—"

"No, I'm serious. I was a complete ass for making you drive when I should have—"

Angie reached over and pressed her fingers against his lips, effectively silencing him. He ignored the excitement he felt at just that little bit of contact, enjoying instead the sight of her broad smile.

"Jay, you should probably get up before people thinking you're proposing or something."

"What?" He pulled away so quickly that he nearly lost his balance and fell on the floor. It was only then that he realized he had dropped to one knee. He turned his head and noticed several of the patrons, and even the wait staff, watching them with smiles.

"Holy shit." He scrambled back to his chair and sank it into it, wishing he could sink into the floor instead. But the embarrassment was worth it when Angie laughed, the sound clear and genuine. He shook his head and reached for his beer, taking a healthy swallow before he joined in her laughter.

"I have no idea what to say right now."

Angie laughed and shook her head. "That makes two of us. But if it makes you feel better, I'll stay for dinner."

"Thank you."

"And you don't have to take me to my car, because I didn't drive down here."

"You didn't? Then how—"

"I took the light rail down then caught a cab from the stadium."

Jay opened his mouth to reply then immediately snapped it shut. Certainly he had misunderstood her. Hadn't he?

"You did what?" His shock must have been clear in his voice because Angie looked up at him in confusion.

"I took the light rail down. I hate driving in the city."

"You took—? Dressed like that?" Jay ignored her careless shrug as anger filled him, anger at himself for not picking her up. To hear she had taken the light rail, a mode of transportation that was iffy at best but damn risky dressed as nicely as she was, upset him on a level that went beyond anger at himself.

"Jay, it was fine. Honest."

He shook his head again. "No, it's not fine. And you are definitely not taking the light rail home tonight."

Angie just smiled at him and said nothing, which was probably for the better because Jay was still steaming. Thoughts of everything that could have happened to her on the way down settled into the pit of his stomach and grew into a sour lump. He took another swallow of beer and muttered to himself.

No, he was definitely taking her home tonight, and at this point, he didn't really care what her brother might say about it.

Chapter Nine

Butterflies swarmed deep in Angie's belly, adding to the feeling of giddiness that threatened to make her giggle. She swallowed the impulse, because she didn't want to giggle.

Not now.

She looked up at Jay, helpless to stop the small smile on her face. He looked more handsome than he had a right to, dressed up as he was. Her eyes drifted down to the open collar of his shirt and she had to curl her fingers into her palm to stop herself from reaching out and running her hand up his chest. It was harder to control the impulse than she thought it would be, not when she already knew how hard and broad that chest was.

He was much more good looking than she first thought, with his dark blonde hair slicked back, not quite brushed completely off his high forehead. And when he watched her with those amazing eyes, like he was now, well, she could almost excuse herself from throwing herself at him that one night.

She wanted to do the same thing right now, but he was so nervous that she was afraid to even move. They were standing at the edge of the front porch, just outside the reach of the front door light. Jay kept glancing around and she knew he was looking for Dave, worried about running into him.

"Thank you again for tonight. I really did have fun."

Jay finally looked down at her, a smile lifting the corners of his mouth and shining in his eyes. "I'm glad. I did, too."

"And you really didn't have to follow me home, you know. I would have been fine by myself." And she would have been. But Jay had insisted on following her after he dropped her off at the light rail station to get her car, and he wouldn't listen to any argument she gave him. And she was secretly glad he did, because that gave them even more time to be together, even if it was only for a few more minutes.

Jay stepped closer to her and her breath caught in her throat. Would he kiss her goodnight? And how silly was that, wishing for a kiss like some teenager? Even so, she couldn't quite hide her disappointment when he merely reached out and tucked a strand of hair behind her ear.

"I know, but I wanted to." His smile faded as he watched her, his eyes serious as he studied her face. The air around them thickened with anticipation and Angie held her breath, wondering if he would kiss her now. He moved forward, just an inch, and suddenly his mouth was on hers, gentle, coaxing.

A small sigh escaped her and she stepped closer, feeling his arms wrap around her waist as his tongue swept across her lips. She slid her hands up his chest and wrapped her arms around his neck, feeling the heat of his body flush against hers as her mouth opened for him, inviting.

The kiss quickly intensified, igniting something deep inside her. The thrust of Jay's tongue became more demanding, coaxing her surrender. She tightened her hold on him and willingly gave in.

Heat coiled inside her, spreading like the fingers of a flame, scorching, burning. Her heart beat heavily in her chest, speeding up under the excitement of his touch. She sighed again, a small sound that was immediately captured by Jay as she pushed herself even closer, wanting, needing to feel all of him.

Jay abruptly broke the kiss and pulled away, just a fraction of an inch. He was breathing heavily and she could see the flush on his face even in the shadows. His eyes studied her, burning in their intensity, searing her nearly as much as his kiss had done.

She expected him to say something. Instead, he cupped her face between his hands and brushed his thumb along her bottom lip. Tingles shot through her at the touch and she opened her mouth in invitation. Jay groaned, a sound of frustration and need, and claimed her mouth once more, walking her backward until she was pressed against the porch post.

He deepened the kiss, demanding a surrender she willingly offered. His body pushed more tightly against hers and she thrust against him, feeling the hard length of his erection against her stomach.

Desire exploded inside her, more intense than she expected. Liquid heat flowed through her, moving with the speed of lava as it consumed her, inch by slow inch. She ran her hands along Jay's shoulders, feeling the hard muscle under her palms. Lower still, down across his open collar. Her trembling fingers found the buttons of his shirt and undid them, one by one, until the shirt was open. She slid her hands inside his shirt, her palms flat against his warm flesh, kneading the solid expanse of muscle. But it wasn't enough, she wanted more, needed to feel all of him.

Jay pulled away and stepped back with a groan, then lowered his forehead against hers. She could see his shaky smile and tried to catch her breath, tried to still her racing heart as she burned on the inside.

"Ang, we need to stop. We can't—"

"Come inside." The invitation came out in a ragged whisper, foreign to her own ears. Jay groaned then leaned forward to give her another kiss, a quick one this time, before shaking his head.

"I want to. You have no idea how much I want to. But Dave—"

"Is working another callback."

Silence greeted her quick reply, and Angie immediately wondered if she should have said anything. She hadn't planned on telling Jay, hadn't thought that tonight would amount to anything.

But it had, and she didn't want it to end.

She could see Jay's mind working, could see him arguing with himself. And she knew that he was still telling himself that it was wrong to be with her. That she was Dave's sister. That there was some kind of stupid manly code of honor that he was breaking.

She held her breath, wondering what he would do. No, she wouldn't throw herself at him again, no matter how much she wanted to. This was something Jay had to resolve on his own.

That didn't mean she had to do stand by and do absolutely nothing.

Angie leaned forward and pressed her mouth against his, nipping at his lower lip before darting her tongue out. His mouth opened immediately under hers, a soft groan escaping him as she pressed herself even closer. She ran her hands along his chest then slowly, reluctantly, pulled away.

He sighed against her mouth, leaning forward for another kiss, but she ducked around him, offering him a small smile.

"I'm going inside if you'd like to join me." She looked at him for another second. A flash of desire crossed his face, followed by something else she couldn't read.

She turned back around and walked to the front door, unlocking it then pushing it open. A smile spread across her face as Jay came up behind her and followed her inside.

**

Jay crossed the threshold and stopped. The silence of the house greeted him, the air inside cool against his flushed skin. Angie reached behind him to close the door and he jumped at the sound of the lock clicking in place. He had a second to wonder if he had just crossed some invisible line before Angie's body brushed against his, and he thought no more.

He grabbed her arm and spun her around, dropping his mouth to hers and claiming her. Devouring her. If he was going to hell for this, then he would gladly burn because it felt right.

She leaned into him, her soft curves pressed against him, her hips fitted just right against his. Her mouth opened for him and he wasted no time in thrusting his tongue into her sweetness. He wanted this. He wanted her. Now.

He pulled away, his eyes searching around him. This wasn't the first time he had been to Dave's—Angie's—house, and he thanked God he knew the layout. He wrapped his hand around Angie's and tugged, leading her through the living room to the stairs, intent only on getting to her room.

Except he wasn't sure which room was hers, and he paused at the stop of the stairs. Angie brushed by him, giving him a small smile, then led him down the hallway, past the bathroom.

And into heaven.

She was in his arms again, her mouth trailing a hot path along his neck, down past his collarbone. He reached between them and yanked at his shirt and jacket, pulling them off and letting them drop to the floor, needing to feel her touch against his skin.

But it wasn't enough. He cupped her face between his hands and claimed her mouth, tasted her surrender. He dragged his hands down along her sides, down past her hips, and grabbed the hem of her dress. Slowly, so slowly, he dragged the material up, exposing her skin to his touch.

She moaned again, nothing more than a soft sigh as he pulled the dress higher, past her waist. He broke the kiss and stepped back, just enough so he could pull the dress over her head, then tossed it to the floor with his shirt.

She stood before him, a wet dream come to life in a lacy thong and matching bra and high heels. His mouth dried up at the sight of her, his breathing ragged as he drank her in. She looked up at him, almost shyly, and he tried to smile but his mind wasn't working, he couldn't focus, could only stare.

"Beautiful."

The word was a harsh whisper, ragged in the heavy air between them, and Jay realized the word had come from him. He let his eyes feast on her, watched the rise and fall of her chest, the fullness of her breasts that were barely restrained by the lacy fabric holding them in place.

He reached out with one finger and traced the line of her collarbone, spread his fingers wider and brought them lower, dipping into her ample cleavage. She grabbed his wrist and for an awful second he thought she was trying to stop him.

But no, she was using him for balance as she leaned down, trying to kick off her heels.

"No." He stopped her with that one word, saw her looking up at him in unspoken question. He shook his head. He swallowed, licked his dry lips. "Leave them on."

Angie straightened and his gut clenched at the expression on her face. Passion, desire, need.

He grabbed her waist in his hands and claimed her mouth once more, guiding her until her back was against the wall. This scene had played out a hundred times or more in his mind.

It was time to witness it in the flesh.

He grabbed both her hands in one of his and pulled them up, holding them above her head as he broke the kiss. Her chest heaved, her heavy breasts spilling over the flimsy material of the bra. His free hand caressed her throat, down lower, her skin flushing under his touch. He pulled at the lace of her bra, freeing her to his gaze.

Her nipples were hard peaks, begging for attention, and he gladly complied. He lowered his mouth to one breast, its weight heavy in his hand as he suckled, teasing her with his tongue, nipping gently with his teeth. Her body shuddered at the touch, her hips thrusting forward to meet air.

He moved to her other breast, tasting and teasing, running his hands down her sides until his fingers hooked into the material of her thong. He looked up at her, at her closed eyes and parted mouth, at the rapid rise and fall of her chest and the heavy beating of the pulse at the base of her neck.

"Beautiful."

He dropped to his knees and pulled her thong down past her hips, her thighs, her knees. Down to her ankles. He raised first one foot, then the other, tossing the material behind him.

And he watched her. Just watched her.

He reached out with one finger and ran it gently up the inside of her calf, the inside of her thigh. Her hands dropped to his shoulders and she spread her legs, opening herself to his gaze.

Jay swallowed, his mouth dry and his mind blank. Need shattered inside him, but he pushed it down, ruthlessly. Not yet.

He leaned forward and dropped his mouth against her wet heat. His tongue flicked out, teasing her clit as he ran one finger between her lips. She was wet, so fucking wet. He slid his finger inside, felt her hips buck against his mouth as she tightened around him, her nails digging into his shoulders.

Not yet.

He smiled against her flesh, the salty tang of her body hot against his tongue.

Then he pulled away and sat back on his heels, looking up at her. Disappointment crossed her face as her eyes fluttered open. She looked down at him.

And he smiled up at her.

"Show me."

Desire flared in her dark eyes as she watched him, hesitating for only a second. Her tongue darted out and licked her parted lips and Jay's gut clenched again, desire and need hardening his cock even more.

But not yet.

Angie lifted her hands from his shoulders, moved them to her neck. Slowly, so slowly, she dragged her hands down her body, her palms skimming her own breasts. She rolled each nipple between her own fingers, squeezing them. Her breathing was shallow and her head fell back with a small moan. Then she spread her fingers and dragged both hands down across her stomach, down further until she touched herself.

She spread her legs even further and leaned against the wall, her hips thrust forward. Light from the small nightlight bathed her with just enough light so he could see her clearly. Jay leaned closer, watching as she held herself open with the fingers of one hand.

Watching as she stroked her clit with one finger, slow at first, teasing.

Her strokes became bolder, harder, faster, unleashing something inside him. His hands closed around her hips and he moved his face closer, still content to watch.

Angie's breathing was ragged now, her tiny moans echoing in the stillness around them as she pleasured herself. Jay slid a finger deep inside her, felt her grip him as her slickness coated his finger. He pulled it out, then slid two in. Out, then in, his rhythm matching her own strokes against her clit.

She tightened again, a hard squeeze around his fingers that made his cock tighten in response. She called his name, a ragged whisper in the air, then shattered. Her hands dropped to his shoulders, her nails digging into his bare flesh. Her hips thrust forward, bucking against his hand, riding his fingers. Jay lowered his mouth to her, his tongue gliding over her clit as she rode her climax hard against his hand.

Now. Fuck, now.

He pulled away from her and stood up, his hands tearing at his pants and pushing them down past his hips. He grabbed her by the waist and lifted her, stepping forward to pin her to the wall as he drove his cock deep inside her.

She tightened around him, saying his name over and over as drove into her, his rhythm harsh and demanding. Her legs tightened around his waist and he felt her mouth against the corded flesh between his neck and shoulder, her teeth nipping and biting.

And damn, he was ready to explode. Now. Felt his balls tighten as her body squeezed his, urging his own release.

"Fuck!" He pulled out of her and held his breath, praying for control. But her hips were still thrusting against him, searching, and he didn't think he could wait much longer, didn't think he could deny his need for another minute.

He shook his head and tried to step away, but Angie's hold around his waist was too strong.

And his willpower too weak.

The need to drive into her, to fill her with his release was overwhelming. Blinding. But he couldn't, not yet.

"Angie, wait." He didn't recognize his own voice

and shook his head, searching deep down for strength. "Condoms, wallet."

A small groan fell from her mouth, her breath hot against his skin. Her legs dropped from his waist and he held onto her as she gained her balance, the feel of her body against his straining cock almost too much to bear.

But instead of standing, instead of letting him get to his wallet, Angie dropped to her knees in front of him. He stood frozen, watching as she looked up at him with a small smile on her face. And shit, fantasies did come true because she closed her mouth around him, a small sigh escaping her as she sucked him.

He stood still, looking down, watching as she ran her tongue along his rigid length, watching as the tip of his cock disappeared into her hot mouth. She leaned forward, taking all of him, her mouth sucking greedily.

He dug his hands into her hair and dropped his head back. Christ, it was too much, he was going to—

He clenched his jaw and tried holding his breath, tried willing her to stop. But his hands were knotted in her hair as his hips thrust forward, driving himself deeper into her hot, wet mouth.

"Angie, stop, I'm going to—"

But he couldn't speak, the words dying in his throat as her hands grabbed his ass and pulled him closer. And shit, he couldn't stop, kept thrusting into her mouth, his hands gripping the back of her head until he exploded.

Seconds went by, sensation rocking him. His breath tore from him on a low groan and he finally looked down, watching Angie suck him, watching her throat move as she swallowed. Another groan escaped him, louder this time, and his knees buckled, bringing him to the floor next to Angie.

She looked up at him and he barely had time to register the brief flash of shyness in her eyes before his mouth closed over hers, hot and demanding. His tongue thrust against her, tasting, savoring.

He pulled away with a groan and stood up, bringing her with him. Neither of them said a word as he led her to the bed and followed her down into the softness of the mattress.

And he was ready again, his cock coming to life as he gazed at her body, flush and welcoming.

He was playing with fire and he didn't care. And if he was going to hell then so be it, because he would gladly burn for Angie.

Chapter Ten

Angie spun on her heel and reached for the bottle of tequila but bumped into Rick instead. The glass fell from her hand and smashed against the hard floor, drawing a chorus of "ooooooooos" from the crowd. Angie cussed under her breath and stepped around the broken glass, grabbing the broom and dustpan from the back corner behind the bar.

"Slow down girl, you're entirely too distracted."

"Yeah, sorry." Angie swept up the glass and dumped the shards into the trashcan then quickly washed her hands. She turned back and grabbed another glass, starting over again.

Distracted wasn't quite the right word, but she wasn't going tell Rick that. She was just glad the crowd was manageable instead of overwhelming—she could only imagine how flustered she'd be then.

But even flustered wasn't quite the right word. Excited, tired, energized. Excited. Definitely excited.

She still couldn't believe more than two weeks had gone by since her dinner date with Jay. She had expected—had been afraid—that she wouldn't see him again. Tried to tell herself it would for the best. But the exact opposite had happened.

Instead of not seeing Jay again, there had been two weeks of quiet phone calls, lasting hours as they just talked, getting to know each other. Two weeks of meeting for a quick lunch while she was working at the clinic, or for quick dinners afterwards. More than two weeks of laughter as she discovered his sense of humor, his relaxed way of looking things, his ability to be so even-keeled over just about anything.

And more than two weeks of intense, mind-blowing, earth-shattering intimacy. Jay may be relaxed and even-keeled about almost everything—except in bed. And while they didn't spend every night together—they couldn't, not with his work schedule, not with hers, and certainly not with her brother—they made use of every moment they were given.

Memories of last night brought a smile to her face and sent heat rushing through her, and she was certain her cheeks were flushed. She tried to wipe the grin from her face as she finished the margarita and placed it on the bar next to the other drinks.

The guest placed a large bill on the counter then left with his drinks, and Angie figured she probably hadn't done a very good job controlling her smile. Yeah, no doubt the guy had thought she was trying to flirt with him or something.

She rang up his tab then tossed the remaining bills in the tip jar before taking a sip of her soda. Yes, she was definitely distracted, flustered, tired. Excited.

Funny how just the memory of her time with Jay could have that effect on her. But not even the excitement of the memories could dispel her tiredness, and she had to stifle the yawn that was trying to break free.

To say she hadn't slept much the last two weeks or so would be putting it mildly. She had worked at the clinic today, and had two hours to spare before her shift at the bar started. The two hours had been spent wisely and she had managed a quick nap, but not much more.

Motion from the corner of her eye caught her attention and she looked over. Her smile broadened and she walked over, leaning across the bar as Jay leaned forward.

"Hey."

"Hey, yourself." Neither of them said anything else, they just stood there watching each other. Jay grinned and leaned a little closer and Angie wondered if he would actually kiss her, right there at the bar.

His gaze dropped to her mouth and she held her breath, waiting. But his grin only broadened as he looked back into her eyes.

She cleared her throat and looked down, trying to tame the burn that just his look caused. "So, what would you like?"

"Hm. I don't think you're serving what I want right now."

"No?"

"Definitely not." Desire flashed in his eyes and she felt the flame curl higher in her stomach as he pinned her with a smoldering look. Angie wished she could offer some witty comeback, some sexy response, but all she could do was grin at him.

He cleared his throat and leaned back just a bit, putting some space between them. He glanced over his shoulder and she followed his gaze, her eyes resting on the guys from his shift.

Including her brother, Dave.

She swallowed her sigh of frustration and turned back to Jay, noticing the same look of frustration on his face.

"Well, since I can't have what I really want right now, how about another round?"

Angie smiled then busied herself with pulling the assorted beers from the cooler. She arranged them on a tray then passed it to Jay. His hand brushed against hers when he grabbed it, his touch warm and lingering against her fingers before he finally straightened.

He lowered his gaze to her mouth once more, then offered her another smile and a slow wink. She swallowed, her gaze hungry as she watched him walk away.

"Need me to hose you down?"

"What?" She turned to face Rick, not really catching his words. He raised his eyebrows in question as he glanced at the spot Jay had occupied before looking back at her.

"I said, do you need me to hose you down? Maybe throw you in the cooler?"

"Was it that obvious?"

"Let's put it this way: I was tempted to pour ice down your back just to see how fast it would boil."

"Shit." Angie shook her head and busied herself with straightening behind the bar. Had she been that obvious? Yeah, she had been. And if Rick had noticed, that meant anyone else could have noticed.

"Don't worry, I could have poured ice over his head and gotten the same reaction."

She knew Rick was trying to comfort her, trying

to reassure her that the entire encounter—that her reaction to it—wasn't one-sided. But that wasn't the problem.

The problem was her pig-headed, over-protective brother and what he would do if he found out.

"So. Doesn't he work with your brother?" Angie moaned, not surprised that Rick knew who everyone was. Of course he knew—he was the main bartender, he knew everyone who came in here.

And it wasn't like Dave and Jay and the rest of their shift never came in here. No, they were pretty much regulars, along with all the other firemen and paramedics that came in. There was no sense in lying to Rick, so she let out a deep breath and nodded.

"Yeah. Yeah, he does."

"And I take it Dave doesn't know?"

"No, Rick, he doesn't know. And I'd like to keep it that way."

Rick held his hands up, mocking surrender as he laughed. "Easy girl. I'm not about to tell you what you can and can't do. But if you want to make sure he doesn't find out, you need to tone it down some."

"Okay, yeah. Thanks."

She offered him a smile to let him know she really did appreciate his advice, then moved to wait on another customer. The next hour passed in much the same fashion, with lulls between customers and what she hoped were inconspicuous glances between her and Jay. It was during one of these glances—which was probably too long to be considered a glance—that she felt a sharp jab in her side. She rubbed her hand along her ribs and shot Rick a dirty look.

"What was that for?"

"Just a heads-up." He nodded over her shoulder and she turned around, expecting to see Dave glowering at her. Instead her eyes came to rest on Todd, and she didn't bother hiding her groan. Rick looked at her, silently asking if she wanted him to wait on her ex, but she shook her head then walked over to where he was standing.

"What do you want?"

"You must not make much in tips if you treat all your customers this way." Todd's comment drew a laugh from his two friends but she ignored them, facing Todd with one hand on her hip and a plastic smile on her face.

"What I do or don't make isn't any of your business, Todd. Now do you want something to drink or not?"

"Yeah, give us three Jager Bombs."

Angie rolled her eyes, not surprised that his drink choice reflected his maturity. She moved to the second cooler and grabbed two cans of energy drinks, then filled three pint glasses halfway full before pouring three chilled shots. She took everything back over and placed the drinks on the bar.

"Do you want to start a tab or pay now?"

"No, we'll definitely start a tab."

She started to turn away but Todd grabbed her wrist and pulled her back. "So who's the guy?"

"What guy?"

"That guy over there, the one who keeps watching you. The one who was here with you last month."

Angie pulled her wrist from his hand and stepped back, fixing him with a glare that he completely ignored. "I have no idea what you're talking about."

She moved to the other side of the bar and chatted with some other customers, pouring drinks and pulling bottles from the cooler. The place between her shoulder blades began itching, and she knew it was because Todd was watching her every move. She tried to ignore him, ignore the laughter and loud comments his friends were making.

What had she ever seen him? She still couldn't believe they had dated, even if it had only been for a few weeks. And she didn't understand why he was suddenly showing up here, months after she had broken it off with him.

"I need to go in the back real quick. You going to be okay out here?"

She looked up at Rick, surprised at his question, then realized he was watching Todd and his friends. Angie rolled her eyes. "Yeah, I'm fine. They're assholes, but they're harmless."

"Okay. Holler if you need me."

Angie smiled her appreciation, then grimaced when Todd called her over.

"Another round, babe."

"I'm not your 'babe', so cool it."

She turned her back on him and busied herself with making another round. She noticed Jay watching her in concern and she gave him a small smile to let him know she was fine. Then she took the drinks back to Todd and started collecting the empty glasses.

Before she could stack them together and grab them, Todd reached out and snagged her left wrist, his grip tighter this time.

"No, don't go. I want to talk to you."

"Todd, get off me." She tried pulling out of his grip but his hand closed more tightly around her, pulling her closer until she was forced to lean across the bar. She clenched her jaw and yanked again. "Todd, I mean it. Get off."

"C'mon Angie, I just want to talk. I missed you."

She shook her head and pulled, but still couldn't get away from him. She reached out and closed her free hand over his and tried prying his fingers off, but his grip tightened even more. Her breath escaped in a hiss as pain shot up her arm and she looked up at Todd, suddenly worried. His eyes were glazed, his mouth turned down in a frown as he stared at her.

"Angie, I just want to spend time with you. C'mon, stop playing hard to get."

"Todd, you're hurting me." Her words came out in a low hiss, from shock and pain as the bones in her wrist ground together.

"Let her go. Now."

Angie looked over, relief filling her when she saw Jay walking over, his long gait rapidly closing the distance between them. His fists were clenched by his side and a feral look glowed in his eyes. And Angie had thought he was relaxed and even-keeled? Not now, not with the danger thrumming through his tense body. Angie looked behind him and saw he wasn't alone, that several other guys were now bearing down on them.

Todd released his hold on her wrist. But Angie's relief quickly turned to dismay when he stood up, so quickly his stool slid back. His two friends joined him, but at least they had the sense to look worried. This could get out of hand so quickly and she needed to do something before it did. She turned and looked for Rick but didn't see him, so she hurried around the bar and stepped between Todd and Jay—and Jay's coworkers.

"Todd, you need to leave. Now."

"I'm not going anywhere."

Why wouldn't he listen? Was he so stupid that he couldn't see the trouble that was brewing directly in front of him? She blew out a heavy sigh and shoved her hair out of her face, then reached out to touch him on the shoulder.

Except Todd was drunk and instead of just standing there, he must have taken it as some kind of invitation because he wrapped his arms around her and pulled her close against him.

"Todd, enough. Leave." She pushed against his chest but he ignored her.

"Come with me, Angie. We can catch up."

Angie was suddenly pulled backwards, hard enough to break the hold Todd had around her waist. She stumbled and nearly fell, catching herself at the last minute by grabbing the edge of the bar with her left hand.

She ignored the flare of pain that shot through her wrist and looked around, trying to get her bearings. There was a flurry of movement in front of her, several flashes and quick grunts. A fuzzy reminder popped into her mind, a warning Rick had given her when she first started working here: never get in the middle of a bar fight. Angie quickly stepped back, moving away.

But it wasn't a bar fight. Or if it was, it was the shortest bar fight in history, over before it really even began. Rick had hold of Todd by his arm and was leading him none too gently toward the door. Todd's friends followed, walking more slowly, as if they were afraid to get too close.

Funny, but she hadn't even seen Rick come out from the back. And now she wondered how much trouble she'd get in for what just happened, for not being able to control it.

She let out a deep breath and shook her hand, wincing at the stab of pain in her wrist. Just what she didn't need.

"Here, let me look."

Jay was suddenly beside her, one arm wrapped around her shoulders in a comforting hug as he took her wrist in his hand. She fought the urge to drop her head on his shoulder, surprised at how suddenly she had started shaking, like she was outside in subzero temperatures.

She tried pulling her wrist from his hand but didn't have the energy, not when his hand was so warm. His entire body was warm and she stepped closer, trying to quell her sudden shivering. His arm tightened around her shoulder.

"Are you okay?" His voice was soft against her ear. She looked up at him and tried to give him a small smile.

"Yeah, I'm fine. Really."

The look in his eyes intensified, warming her as much as the heat from his body, and she leaned even closer to him. She felt his lips brush against her temple before he gently lifted her wrist. She tried not to wince as his body went rigid next to hers, jolting her arm, and she figured she must not have done a very good job of hiding that brief flare of pain.

Angie looked up, ready to reassure him that she was fine, but finally noticed that he wasn't looking at her—or her wrist. He was looking off to her side, his jaw clenched, some of the color draining from his face.

And that's when she remembered they weren't alone. That they were in a bar—the bar where she worked—and that Jay was here with his shift.

With her brother.

She stiffened and turned her head in the direction Jay was looking, the breath catching in her throat sharply enough to make her choke.

Dave was less than a foot away, his expression hard as he stared at both of them with fury in his dark eyes.

"What the hell are you doing with my sister?"

Chapter Eleven

"Dammit, Moore, I want an answer. Now."

The demand echoed around the engine room, bounced off the equipment, and came back to ring in Jay's ears. He clenched his jaw and stepped away from Dave, knowing it didn't matter how loud the man got.

Everyone in the station already knew exactly what was going on. Maybe not exactly. But they knew something was going, no doubt picking up on the tension that had settled over the station since the start of their shift. Not to mention the yelling.

Jay had to give them credit, though, because nobody was asking questions or paying them much attention. At least, not anymore.

Because the entire confrontation had been going on all day, interrupted by medic calls and fire calls. It was nearly shift change, and Jay really hoped for another call just so he could avoid what was coming.

But it looked like his luck had just ran out.

"Dave, I told you before, I'm not getting into this with you. Not now, and especially not here."

"Bullshit. This is my sister we're talking about."

"Is it? You sure you're not more worried about yourself?"

"Cut the crap. This has nothing to do with me, and everything to do with Angie."

"Then what did she tell you?"

"That's none of your damned business."

Jay wondered if Dave was telling him what he thought—or what Angie had told him. Seeing how Dave had been acting all day, he imagined it was probably a little bit of both.

And dammit all to hell, anyway. If he hadn't been so stupid last night, this wouldn't even be happening. But he had seen that asshole grab her and he nearly lost it. If Rick hadn't shown up to toss the guy and his friends out, there was no telling what might have happened.

And not just with Jay, with all of them. Including Dave. Because everyone had suddenly been in a mood to fight after seeing what had happened.

And even that would have been fine, if it had ended there. But Angie had looked upset and Jay hadn't even stopped to think, just immediately went over to comfort her. Putting his arm around her shoulders had been instinct, dropping a kiss on her temple had been instinct. He hadn't even thought about where he was or who else was there, he had just acted.

And now the shit had just gotten real.

Jay walked over to the engine and made himself look busy, opening cabinets, checking tools, whatever he could find. But Dave followed him.

"Dave, I am not getting into this."

"You don't have a choice. I want to know what

the hell is going on between you and Angie."

"Nothing, Dave. Okay? Nothing. Now will you just get the hell away from me?"

"It didn't look like nothing last night."

"Christ Dave, she was upset and I gave her a hug. That's it. Let it go." Jay's own temper was bubbling to the surface and he needed to get away, quick. Yeah, he understood Dave's anger, even sympathized with it, which made the entire scenario that much worse.

Because this was exactly what Jay had been afraid would happen.

The worst part of it was that he wasn't sorry. Yeah, he sympathized with Dave's anger, but that didn't mean he was going to take any more of his harassment so he turned away, intent on just walking away.

Dave grabbed him by the shoulder and spun him around. "I'm not done with you, Moore."

Jay's temper frayed and he pushed Dave's hand from his shoulder, stepping back as he did so. "Dave, I said let it go."

Dave's face was red with fury and he took a step closer, his finger nearly hitting Jay in the chest. Jay clenched his jaw and took another step back, certain his own face was nearly as red as Dave's.

"Are you fucking my sister?"

Jay didn't even think, just plowed straight into Dave with both arms outstretched, pushing him into the side of the engine. Noise exploded in the engine room around them but Jay ignored it, ignored the hands that were grabbing his arms, ignored the bodies that were suddenly between Dave and him.

"Who the hell do you think you are? You don't talk about your sister like that!"

"She's my sister! If I find out you so much as touched her—"

"Go to hell!"

"Knock it off. Both of you!"

Mike stepped between them, separating them with one hand on each of their chests. Her face was flushed with anger and she took turns giving them both a dirty look. Hands tugged at his shoulders again and he turned to see Jimmy behind him, pulling him back. He shrugged off the man's hold then straightened his shirt, staring at Dave.

His brows were lowered in a severe frown, his dark eyes glinting with anger. He pushed Mike's hand away from his chest and stepped to the side, his eyes never leaving Jay's. He raised one hand and pointed his finger in Jay's direction.

"Stay the hell away from sister!"

"Fuck you!"

"Dammit, Jay, enough!" Mike grabbed his arms and pulled him to the rear of the engine as Jimmy started after Dave.

"I'll go try to calm him down."

Mike rolled her eyes after him, then turned back to Jay, her expression stern. She finally shook her head and pushed Jay toward the back step. He caught himself before he tripped, then slowly sat down, still breathing heavy.

"I don't want to hear it, Mikey."

She looked at him with feigned shock. "Who, me?" She sat sideways on the back step, pulling one knee into her chest while the other swung back and forth. Neither one of them said anything for a minute and Jay was thankful for the brief silence so he could gather his thoughts.

"So what's going on, Jay? Are you dating Angie?"

"We've been seeing each other for a couple of weeks, yeah."

"And?"

Jay turned to face her and saw the unasked question in her eyes: was he sleeping with her? He didn't say anything, but she must have seen the answer on his face anyway because she let out a long breath and shook her head.

"What are you going to do now?

"About what?"

Mike raised her brows in his direction then waved her arm around. "About this. About Dave."

"Damn if I know." Jay rubbed his hands across his face then leaned his head back. That was the problem right there—he really didn't know what he was going to do. They were more than coworkers, they were friends. Family. Or rather, they had been friends. And he no idea what to do now.

"What about Angie?"

"What about her?"

Mike studied him in silence, her face carefully blank. She was quiet for so long that Jay wondered if he missed something. But Mike just shook her head and dropped her gaze on a sigh.

"What I meant was: are you going to see her again, or are you going to move on?"

"What the hell kind of question is that?"

"Jay, I love you dearly so don't take this the wrong way but—you don't exactly have a reputation for long-term relationships."

"Really, Mike? Thank you so much. You know, I'd expect something like that coming from any of the other guys but not you. So thanks." He moved, fully intending to stand up and walk away, but was stopped by Mike's hand on his arm.

"Jay, that's not how I meant it and you know it."

He brushed her hand off but didn't move. "No, I don't."

"Jay, this is me you're talking to, okay? How many times have you said yourself that you're not interested in a relationship? That you have 'encounters', not 'dates'?" Her voice was quiet, understanding. Not judging, just stating fact. But it still upset him to hear his own words thrown back at him. And if it had been anyone besides Mikey saying it, he would have stormed off and taken his aggressions out on the punching bag downstairs in the gym.

But it *was* Mikey. And they *were* his words.

He shook his head, not sure what to say. No, he had no interest in a relationship. He tried that once and it hadn't ended well, and he had never looked back. He had also never looked forward, never thought about looking forward. He was quite happy just living day-to-day.

And Mikey, of all people, knew that. Which was the only reason he didn't say anything.

"So, about Angie. Is she just another encounter?"

"No." Jay shook his head. "No, she's not." And it was the truth. He wanted to keep seeing her, liked just being around her. And he wanted to keep getting to know her better. He had no idea where things would lead, just knew that he liked being around her. Liked being with her. Why did that have to be so terrible?

Mike watched him, her head tilted to one side as she studied him. "Jay, are you sure you're not interested in her just because...I mean, it's not a case of forbidden fruit, is it?"

"Christ Mikey, really?"

She leaned back and held her hands out in surrender, but the small grin on her face let him know that she wasn't really worried about upsetting him.

But was she right? Was this attraction to Angie nothing more than wanting something he wasn't supposed to have? He closed his eyes, recalling Angie's face and her smile. Her laughter. The sound of her voice when they talked for hours. He shook his head. No, if it was a case of wanting something he couldn't have, he mostly certainly wouldn't be thinking about her face or her voice. And if it was a case of wanting something he couldn't have, well, he certainly wouldn't have gotten so pissed off last night. And he certainly wouldn't be worrying about when he could see her again.

He opened his eyes and looked over at Mike, shaking his head in answer to her question. "No, it's not a case of forbidden fruit. I like her, Mikey. Why does that have to be a bad thing?"

"I never said it was. I just want to make sure you know what you're getting into, especially with Dave. You're going to have to sit down and talk to him, Jay, regardless. And if you keep seeing Angie without talking to him? Well, things could get even uglier."

"Yeah. Yeah, I know."

She stood up and stretched, then punched him in the shoulder as she walked by. "Call me if you need to talk."

Jay watched her leave, knowing she was right. He needed to talk to Dave. But what was he supposed to say? And what about Angie? For all he knew, she might not be interested in seeing him again, especially if Dave had given her half as bad a hard time as he had given Jay.

And that thought worried the hell out of him.

Chapter Twelve

A light breeze blew through the open window. The sheer curtains billowed into the room, letting more of the early evening sun into the room. Angie twisted her head to the side and thought about getting up to pull the shade.

She didn't have the energy.

And her wrist hurt.

Of course, if she hadn't been holding the e-reader in her left hand, her wrist wouldn't hurt as much as it did. But she had nothing better to do today, and wanted to just laze around and enjoy a quiet Sunday. So far, she had been successful.

If you didn't count all the times she had looked at her phone, wondering if Jay would call.

Or if she should call him.

Which wasn't really fair, because he had called her once, earlier in the day, to check on her and make sure she was okay. And then they had just talked. Not about anything in particular, just comfortable conversation, getting to know each other a little more.

That didn't mean she didn't want to talk to him again, though. She laughed at herself. She really was acting like a teenager when it came to Jay, and she wasn't sure why.

The sound of a car pulling into the driveway drifted through the window and Angie held her breath, listening. She winced at the sound of his truck door slamming and knew that any peace and quiet she might have been enjoying was coming to end.

Her brother was home, and from the sound of the front door slamming as well, he wasn't in a good mood.

Not that that surprised her, considering the mood he had been in last night. But it had been too late when she got home last night for anything more than a brief argument, stopped short when she slammed her bedroom door in his face. It was too much to hope there wouldn't be a full interrogation now.

Her ears traced the sound of Dave's heavy footsteps through the house. Through the dining room and into the kitchen, back through to the living room to the stairs and up. And finally to the hallway, stopping outside her door.

Dave leaned against the doorjamb, his dark eyes watching her. He didn't bother coming in, just stood right outside the door and stared at her. His jaw was clenched tight, stress deepening the lines around his eyes and mouth. She was suddenly surprised to realize how attractive he was, with his large frame, square jaw, and deep-set eyes. And she wondered why he never really dated, at least that she knew of. Or why he never did more than hang out with his friends from work.

He used to, years ago. Going to this party or that, dating here and there. Nothing serious. But not lately. In fact, he hadn't really done much socializing at all since he had come back from his deployment with the Reserves two years ago, and she didn't know why she had never realized that before.

She studied him in the quiet that fell between them. And for a brief second, Angie thought he looked...older. More tired. She blinked and the thought disappeared, helped along by her pushing it from her mind.

She didn't want to think of her brother as vulnerable, didn't want to think about him with any kind of sympathy. Not when she knew the interrogation was getting ready to start.

"I want you to quit working at the bar." His voice was flat, steady, and left no room for argument. It hadn't been the first thing she expected to hear from him, but she still wasn't surprised.

And she didn't bother to answer, just shook her head and pretended to turn her attention back to the e-reader.

"Angela, that wasn't a request. You're quitting."

"Or what? You're going to lock me in my room?"

"It's too dangerous. Last night proved that."

"Oh please. Last night was a fluke. Todd was drunk. If you and your friends hadn't overreacted, things would have been fine." Angie inwardly winced as the words left her mouth. Why had she mentioned his friends? She had just given him the perfect opening to the conversation she least wanted to have.

"Speaking of my friends." She didn't miss the heavy sarcasm in the word. "Stay away from Jay. He's no good for you."

Angie pushed herself to a sitting position but stopped herself from completely standing. If she did, she'd just go over and slam the door in Dave's face. And as much as she didn't want a confrontation, she knew it was coming. The longer they put it off, the worse it would be.

"You have to stop telling me what to do, Dave. I'm not a little kid. I don't need you to tell me what's good for me."

"Somebody needs to because you sure as hell can't figure it out on your own!" He snapped his mouth shut, the shout still ringing in the room. He stared at her then shook his head. "Dammit, Angie, the man has a string of women in his wake. He can't keep it in his pants, and once he has something, he moves on to the next one. Can't you see I'm just trying to save you some heartache?"

A sharp pain twisted through her stomach at the words, like someone had just shoved a knife deep inside her gut. But she pushed it away, refusing to let Dave's accusation color her judgment. Yes, she had known Jay dated a lot of different women, just from watching him bring a few of them to the bar. That didn't mean he was using her.

Especially since she was the one who had thrown herself at him. But she wasn't about to tell her brother *that*.

"Dave, it's not up to you. This is my life, you need to let me live it."

"Not when it's so obvious that you can't be trusted to make the right decisions."

"Really? You can stand there and accuse me of that?" She pushed herself from the bed and closed the distance between them with a few angry steps. "How can you even say that? I'm twenty-four years old, Dave. I have a bachelor's in Animal Sciences that I got on a full ride scholarship! I'm finishing my third year at Vet school, and I'm working and putting myself through it. And I'm doing it by myself, just like I did everything myself for eighteen months while you were gone! So don't sit there and tell me I can't be trusted to make the right decisions!"

Dave stepped back, shock at her outburst clear in his eyes. Shock, and something else. Surprise? Or hurt? No, she refused to think that anything she had said could hurt him.

He stared at her, then leaned forward the barest inch, just enough to make her step back. Anger tightened his face and laced his voice when he spoke. "You are still my sister and if I see you making a mistake, I will damn well tell you, and then do everything I can to make sure you don't. And I'm telling you, Jay is a mistake. Now stay away from him."

He turned on his heel and stormed away, his steps heavy on the stairs. The front door slammed and a minute later she heard his truck start, rubber squealing against the blacktop driveway as he left.

Angie didn't move for a long minute. Her heart pounded in her chest and something sour rolled in her stomach. From their fight? She thought so. She couldn't remember the last time they had shouted at each other like that, if they ever had.

Dave was her brother, the only close family she really had. They had picked up the pieces together after their father took off, almost ten years ago. In a lot of ways, Dave had almost been like a father to her, getting her through those rough high school years, worrying about her dating, giving her a shoulder to cry on when the guy she wanted to go to prom with asked someone else instead.

Then he had left, called to active duty for eighteen months, and Angie had been alone again—but she was older, more than capable of handling everything herself. Part of her worried that Dave felt guilty for leaving her, which made no sense to her even though she knew her brother well enough to understand why he'd feel that way.

And when he came back, he tried to act like nothing had changed. But she knew. She could tell. He wasn't quite the same. A little quieter, a little more reserved—and entirely too quick to assume responsibility for everything and everyone else. *Too* worried, *too* protective. It was almost like he felt he had to be, to make up for the time he'd been gone. But even then, they were still close, still leaned on each other. They were still a family, arguments and all.

She didn't like the thought that anything could come between them, not after everything they'd been through. She walked back to the bed and sat on the edge, her hand pressed against her middle.

Was that why he'd said all those things about Jay? Was he just being overly protective again? Worrying too much? Or was it something more? Was it something he knew that she didn't?

She pressed her hand more tightly against her stomach and took a deep breath, trying to calm the sour twisting that was slowly rising inside her. And she wondered if the awful twisting feeling in her stomach was from the fight with Dave—or from the awful things he had said about Jay.

Chapter Thirteen

"What the hell? Are you trying to fucking kill me?"

Jay lowered the axe, pulling down a piece of damaged drywall with it. He turned his head to the side and spit the blackened mucus from his mouth then looked over his shoulder at Mikey. She was standing just behind him, her mask hanging loose around her neck, her brows lowered in a frown as she stared at him.

"What?"

"You damn near took my head off with the axe. Get your head on straight and watch what you're doing." She stepped around him and moved deeper into the room, kicking at the pile of burnt debris littering the floor. Jay blinked, not quite sure he heard her right.

"Really? You're really going to go there with me? After all your shit last year with Nick?"

Mike looked over her shoulder at him, a small grin tilting the corners of her mouth. The look was completely at odds with her sweat and soot-stained face. "Of course. Why would you expect anything different from me?"

Jay grunted, not knowing what to say. Of course he shouldn't expect anything different. Why would he? He shook his head and swung the axe, listening as it hit the wall with a solid thunk. He pulled down, tearing away more of the wall.

"So what's going on with you two?"

Jay swung the axe again then let it drop to his side. "With what two?"

"Don't play dumb, Jay. You know exactly who I'm talking about."

Yeah, he did. That didn't mean he wanted to discuss it, not even with Mikey. And especially not here on the fire ground, where any number of people might overhear. "Nothing's going on."

Mike swore behind him, the words harsh and disbelieving. A second later and she was standing next to him, leaning one shoulder against the wall and staring at him with those clear blue eyes that always saw too much. Gone was any trace of a smile, any sign of humor. This was Michaela being serious, something he wanted to avoid at all costs.

"Is it getting serious between you two?"

"What?" He frowned then shook his head, thought about giving her a short little laugh to go along with his look of disbelief. Jay swallowed back the laugh, nearly choking, and shook his head again. "Serious? Me? Of course not."

Which is what he knew Mike was expecting him to say. He could see that much in her eyes. He could also see her unspoken words, the ones where she called him a liar. Yeah, he heard that loud and clear even without her saying it. He turned his head to the side and spit again, not quite able to meet her stare.

"You know I'm calling bullshit, right?"

"Yeah, whatever Mikey."

"Hey, don't get an attitude with me. Best friend, remember? I'm not the one who has a problem with it. And I told you before, I like Angie."

"And now you're wondering how long before I screw her over, right?" Jay took a step to the side, half-expecting Mike to slug him for the words he already regretted saying. No, Mike wouldn't expect him to do that, no matter what everyone else might think.

But she didn't say anything, just stood there with her arms crossed, looking both lethal and thoughtful in the dirty turnout gear and bottle. She uncrossed her arm and dragged her wrist across her forehead, leaving a smear of soot and grime on her face. To her credit—and his surprise—she ignored the comment completely and walked over to the other side of the room, tearing at the wall in the corner.

"Nick and I are going out for dinner and a movie tomorrow night. Why don't you guys join us?"

He almost said yes. The idea of going on a date, hanging with friends who would accept them and not judge, was more tempting than he imagined. But he shook his head, giving Mike a small smile as he did.

"We already made plans." His grin grew a little wider as he thought about where he was taking her. Mike raised her brows, no doubt thinking he had something else entirely in mind.

"Is that so?"

"Shut up. That's not what I meant." He leaned to the side and looked out the door through the thinning haze to make sure nobody else was around. "I'm taking her to the carnival."

"Really?" Mike laughed then quickly stopped, clearing her throat when he shot her a dirty look.

"What's wrong with that?"

"Nothing. Honest. It's actually kind of sweet. I wouldn't have expected that from you."

"Sweet?" Great. That wasn't exactly the result he'd been aiming for. "Is it too silly? Maybe I should—"

"Jay, stop. I think it's a good idea. You guys will have fun."

"Are you sure? I haven't told her yet, so it's not too late—"

"Man, you really do like her, don't you?"

It wasn't so much a question as it was a statement but it still caught him off-guard. If not the words, then definitely the way she said it—like it was a sure thing, not even up for debate. He shouldn't be surprised, though. It was nothing less than what he would have expected from Mike. Maybe that was the issue: because it was Mike, and he wouldn't lie to her.

And because she was right. He did like Angie. More than he expected. She wasn't like the other women he'd dated. That in itself was a whole other problem. In the past, he dated women closer to his own age, even a little older. Women who weren't looking for relationships. Women who were completely comfortable with what he had to offer—which was a few nights of fun and not much else.

Angie was younger, by six years—something he tried not to think too hard about. Was she looking for a relationship? He couldn't say, but he was pretty damn sure that she wasn't the kind of woman who was fine with just a few nights of pleasure. And oddly enough, that was fine with him because he suddenly wanted more. He was done with the casual encounter thing, done with the dating scene, done with all of it.

But with Angie? Yeah, he liked her. Liked being with her. Loved her smile and laughter and the way she made him feel. And he loved her sense of family loyalty, even if her ass of a brother didn't deserve it.

Which wasn't fair. He and Dave used to be close, used to be friends. Yeah, that had definitely changed. And while Jay could understand Dave's feelings, at least a little bit, he still thought the man was overreacting.

"Yo. Earth to Jay." Mike's voice was right next to his ear and he turned, startled, just as she nudged him. He stumbled into the wall and automatically brought his hand up to catch himself. The wall crumbled and his hand shot through, throwing him off-balance even more.

"Dammit." He jerked his arm back and gave Mike a dirty look. "What the hell did you do that for?"

"Me? How was I supposed to know you'd lose your balance? Besides, that's what you get for zoning out so much." She pulled some more of the wall down then looked behind it, searching for more extension before looking at him over her shoulder. "What were you thinking about?"

"Do you think Dave is overreacting? Or am I really that big of a dick?"

Mike stared at him for a few seconds then let out a long sigh. She lowered her head and pinched the bridge of her nose, then shook her head. "Lord save me from stupid men."

"What? I think that's a valid question."

"And you really want the answer?"

"Yeah, I do."

"Okay." She paused, watching him, her expression suddenly too serious. "Yes. To both questions. Dave is overreacting and you can be a dick. Happy?"

"No."

"Then you shouldn't have asked." She stepped forward and gave his shoulder a small push before smiling. "Listen, Jay. You've had your moments. So have I. You remember all the shit I gave Nick last year? Nobody's perfect. Do I think you're going to be a dick with Angie? No. You're different with her. More…I don't know. Relaxed. More yourself. I think you guys make a cute couple."

"So you think he's overreacting? Or do you think he has a point?"

Mike watched him for a long minute, her clear gaze too serious, too intense. Then she shook her head and swung the axe once more, hitting high on the wall and tearing down a chunk of drywall. Once, twice. Once more. Jay swallowed back his disappointment, certain that her silence meant she thought that Dave was right, that whatever was going on between Angie and him didn't have a snowball's chance in hell of working out.

And dammit, that pissed him off. Hell, he'd be the first to admit that his history wasn't the greatest. Yeah, he had a reputation for not settling down. A reputation for playing the field, for dating too many women. But not at once. Fuck no, never that. He'd been on the receiving end of that shit and would never even think about doing that to someone else.

And he never used women. Never treated them bad. So why the hell was Mikey so silent? And why did he feel like her silence was so damned accusing?

"Yes and no."

"What?"

Mike dropped the axe to her side and gave Jay a sideways look, the corner of her mouth tilting ever so slightly. "I said yes and no. Yeah, I think Dave is overreacting and no, I don't think he has a point."

She rested her shoulder against the wall, still watching him—too carefully, studying him too much. "Angie's his little sister. He's going to be protective, that's to be expected. But there's something else going on with him."

"Yeah, okay."

"No, really. He hasn't been himself. Haven't you noticed that?"

Jay barely stopped himself from snorting—or from saying something out loud that would end being overheard even out on the street. "No, I haven't noticed. I've been a little busy avoiding getting into a fight with him."

"Don't be an ass, Jay. Something's been going on even before you and Angie started seeing each other. I can't be the only one who's noticed."

Jay shrugged, not wanting to think too much about Dave. Yeah, definitely not Dave. But maybe Mike had a point. Maybe, if he stopped to really think, he might agree that something else was going on with Dave.

But he wasn't going to admit it, not even to Mike. And he damn sure wasn't going to accept that as an excuse for the shit Dave was pulling now. Yeah, Angie was his sister. And yeah, maybe it crossed some imaginary blurred line that Jay was dating her now. But that still wasn't an excuse for Dave's shit. At least, not a valid one, not in Jay's mind.

"Are you two done playing games and gossiping like girls in here?"

Jay turned, surprised to see Adam poking his head around the corner. Something flew through the air, seen from the corner of his eye. He jumped before realizing Mike had thrown a chunk of wet drywall through the air, almost hitting Adam in the chest. The younger man jumped out of the way just in time and grinned.

"Gossiping like a girl? Really, Adam? Don't insult me. You're lucky I didn't throw my axe at you."

"I didn't mean you, Mike. I meant Jay."

"Screw you, Adam. What's the rush, anyway?"

"No rush. Not really. I just want to get back for lunch."

Jay shook his head, resisting the urge to say too much more. Adam was relatively new to their shift, a few years younger than Mike and him. And quiet—almost too quiet. Jay wasn't sure if that was because he was just naturally quiet, or if he was still feeling things out, still trying to find a way to fit in. He didn't want to give him too hard of a time. At least, not yet.

He glanced over at Mike and raised his brows in silent question. She grinned and shrugged, casting a quick glance at Adam before fixing her gaze on Jay. "We're good in here as far as I'm concerned. Anything else you wanted to talk about?"

It didn't matter if he did or not, he sure as hell wasn't going to have any more of this conversation in front of Adam. Not that there was anything he shouldn't have heard—Jay just didn't want everyone else to know too much about his private life. No matter how much of that was currently bleeding over into their station life.

So no, there really wasn't anything else he needed to talk about. He just wanted to spend time with Angie without the hassle of her brother's shit. And maybe that wasn't a realistic expectation. Maybe it never would be. Maybe it wouldn't matter. Maybe Jay was just reading too much into everything, feeling more than he should.

Yeah, wouldn't that just be perfect? After years of never even considering the possibility of settling down, wouldn't it suck if he had the urge to do just that with the one woman he wasn't even supposed to be seeing? Yeah, of course it would. Because that's how life worked.

"Jay?"

"Hm?" He blinked, clearing his mind, and looked up to see Mikey watching him, waiting. Jay blinked once more, struggling to remember the question.

Was there anything else he wanted to talk about? No. No, there wasn't. He'd have to trust whatever was between Angie and him and just take it one day a time, see what happened.

He shook his head and forced a grin to his face. "No, I'm good."

Mikey didn't look like she believed him but she didn't say anything. Good, because he suddenly wasn't in the mood to listen to anything else. He grabbed his axe and looked around the room one last time then followed Mike and Adam out.

Yeah, he could tell himself he was just going to play things by ear, take things day-to-day, all he wanted. That was why all he could think about was tomorrow, when he'd get to see Angie again, get to spend more time with her.

Day-to-day. Sure, no problem.

Chapter Fourteen

Angie's hands gripped the bar in front of her so tightly, she could feel flakes of old paint coming loose against her sweaty palms. She closed her eyes and told herself not to scream, she could not scream. The chair dipped and swayed beneath her before it shuddered and lifted up, and she couldn't help the small squeak that escaped her. And she didn't want to open her eyes, she really didn't, but her stomach was tilting and she knew keeping her eyes closed was making the sensation worse.

So she cracked her eyes open then stiffened as she saw the crowd below her slowly getting smaller.

Jay chuckled and slid closer, draping his arm around her shoulder. The chair dipped and swayed again and Angie tightened her grip even more.

She hated Ferris wheels. Absolutely detested them, had since she was a young girl. And she had no idea why she had agreed to get on this one with Jay.

His arm tightened around her shoulder and he pulled her closer. She took a deep breath and slowly turned her head to look at Jay, felt her breath hitch as he lowered his head and claimed her mouth in a slow lingering kiss. He pulled away and gave her a small smile.

"Better?"

Angie tried to give him a smile but she didn't think she was very effective, not if the expression on his face was any indication. She swallowed, briefly closed her eyes, then opened them and gave him a shaky nod.

"I'll be fine."

"You don't look fine, Angie." He reached over with his free hand and placed it on top of one of hers. Warmth immediately penetrated her skin, and she loosened her grip just a bit. "Why did you agree to get on if you don't like it?"

"Honestly? It's been so long since I've been on one, I forgot how much I hated them." And that was the truth. She had avoided Ferris wheels for years. Give her a rough rollercoaster, a wild spinning ride, or anything that tossed her upside down and side to side. Those rides she could handle, so she had never worried about getting on a Ferris wheel.

Until a few minutes ago, when Jay had suggested they get on this one at the carnival.

"I'm so sorry, Angie." She heard him chuckle and slid him a sideways glance. He squeezed her hand and smiled. "I guess my idea of a romantic ride backfired."

She looked over at him again but didn't say anything, just prayed that the seat would stop swinging. And that the ride would be over soon. Isn't that the way carnivals worked? They charged you an enormous amount for tickets, hyped up the experience, then left you feeling cheated when the ride lasted less than a minute.

And surely a minute had passed already, hadn't it?

She took a deep breath and braved a look over the side, then immediately closed her eyes. They were going around again, the ground falling away beneath them. She knew she should respond to Jay's comment about a romantic ride, but she couldn't, not when she was nearly frozen in terror.

But having him next to her helped. Feeling his arm wrapped around her shoulder, holding her close, and knowing that he had tried to be romantic made the terror just a little more bearable.

She would surely survive this. Just as she had survived Dave's silent treatment for the last three weeks.

And that quick, her melancholy mood resurfaced, pushing away some of the fright caused by the stupid Ferris wheel. She wanted both emotions to disappear, to leave her alone so she could enjoy tonight.

The ride finally stopped and she breathed a heavy sigh of relief, wasting no time in scrambling from the chair once it stopped at the loading platform. She hurried down the ramp, eager to put distance between the ride and her. Jay caught up to her and grabbed her hand, twirling her around so they were face-to-face, her body held tightly against his.

His mouth dropped to hers, the kiss hot and searing, his tongue asserting domination over hers. He pulled away and looked down at her, his gray eyes heated with the same passion she felt blossoming in her.

"I wanted to do that up there but figured it probably wasn't a good idea."

Angie laughed and felt some of the despair she had felt earlier disappear. "No, probably not. Sorry."

Jay grabbed her hand and started walking along the midway. Carnies shouted around them, their voices carrying over the clanging of bells and whistles coming from the games. The sweet scents of cotton candy and funnel cake floated on the light breeze, along with echoes of laughter and screams from the crowd. Angie inhaled deeply, taking it all in as they moved along the midway.

Jay stopped at one of the food carts and ordered funnel cake and lemonade then led them away from the crowd, finding a grassy spot for them to sit, away from the noise and craziness.

Angie lowered herself to the ground and curled her legs under her, smiling a little when Jay sprawled next to her and leaned back on his elbows. The motion caused his shirt to slide up, revealing a slice of sculpted abs between the shirt hem and waist band of his cargo shorts. Angie smiled again, remembering the feel of that warm flesh over a tight stomach beneath her fingers.

"So tell me why you don't like Ferris wheels."

Angie swallowed the bite of funnel cake, feeling it settle like a lump of raw dough in her stomach. The powdered sugar was suddenly too dry, coating her mouth with a too-sweet dust, and she reached for the lemonade. Her earlier enjoyment in their surroundings suddenly dimmed as her thoughts went back to her brother.

Jay must have interpreted her silence wrong, though, because he reached over and ran his hand up her arm, giving her a reassuring squeeze. "Hey, it's no big deal. We all have things we hate, right?"

"Yeah, I guess." She wanted to tell him her sudden silence had nothing to do with her fear of Ferris wheels but he didn't let her finish. Instead, he pushed himself up and shifted so he was sitting closer, the heat of his bare legs brushing up against hers when he moved.

"Okay, I'm going to let you in on a secret. You have to swear you won't tell anyone this because nobody knows, not even Mikey." He reached down and broke off a piece of the funnel cake and popped it into his mouth. He swallowed and looked around, like he was making sure nobody else was around them.

"I hate lizards. They completely freak me out. As in, I might start screaming-like-a-girl freak me out."

Angie just stared at him, not knowing what to say and wondering if he was just being funny. Merriment lit his eyes and the corner of his mouth pulled up in a small grin. She finally shook her head, not believing him. "Lizards? Yeah, right."

He raised his hand, as if swearing an oath. "I shit you not. Can't stand them."

"Lizards? Really? But they're small. And harmless. And they eat bugs."

Jay laughed and took a swallow of his lemonade. "They still freak me out. A friend of mine growing up had a couple of lizards he kept in his room. We were feeding them one day and I guess they must have gotten out or something. Of course, we didn't notice. I was spending the night at his house and felt something cold and slimy on my neck. Turns out it was one of the lizards, getting up close and personal while I slept. Completely freaked me out."

Angie couldn't stop the laughter, even when Jay

gave her a slightly insulted look, as if he couldn't believe she would find his horror amusing. She took a deep breath and tried to apologize, but he shook his head.

"Yeah, it wasn't funny waking up to see those little beady eyes staring at me, and the damn thing's tongue darting out, like he was doing a taste test or something. I screamed like a girl. And to this day, I can't stand even seeing a lizard. Ugh." He gave a mock shudder, which made her laugh again. She grabbed another bite of funnel cake, glad the powdered sugar no longer tasted like dust in her mouth. She looked over at Jay, surprised to find him watching her, his gaze on her mouth. He leaned forward and kissed her, a long slow kiss that stole her breath and ignited a fire inside her.

She brought her hand to his chest, felt the steady beat of his heart against her palm, and leaned in further, wanting to melt against him. But he pulled away too soon, his breathing as shallow as hers.

"You, uh, had some powdered sugar on your lips."

She raised her fingers to her mouth, suddenly self-conscious. Jay smiled at her and tucked a strand of hair behind her ear. "It's all gone now."

"Oh. Thanks." And what a stupid thing that was to say! But Jay just smiled at her again.

"Definitely my pleasure. So what's your story?"

"My story?"

"Yeah. The Ferris wheel. Why don't you like it?"

"Oh, that." Angie looked down, the melancholy returning once more. "It's nothing really. Just something silly that happened a long time ago."

"Sillier than my lizard story? Why don't I believe

that?"

Angie picked at the grass surrounding her, pulling out a long blade. She held it between her fingers, twirling it around before slowly peeling it. She finally let out a sigh and tossed the shredded blade to the side. "Dave and I were on the Ferris wheel once when we were kids, and he thought it would be funny to make the seat rock. Well, I did too, to be honest. But he got it swaying pretty good and I slipped in the seat and thought I was going to fall out, right through the bar. I haven't been much on Ferris wheels since then."

"Great. And I just made you get on one. No wonder you didn't look touched by my romantic gesture." Jay laughed and she knew he was teasing her, but she couldn't seem to find a smile to give him. She pulled up another blade of grass and started peeling it, not wanting him to see the worry in her eyes.

Not wanting him to see a flash of regret.

His hand closed over hers and he leaned forward, tilting his head under hers until she had no choice but to look at him. His gaze was quiet, questioning, and she looked away. "Why do I get the feeling that you're upset about something besides a Ferris wheel?"

"It's nothing, really."

"Talk to me, Ang. Tell me what's going through your mind."

"Honest, it's nothing. It's just—I started thinking about Dave and remembering everything we used to do, and how close we used to be. And now...we're not."

Jay sat back, his expression suddenly blank as he watched her. A long minute went by before he exhaled heavily. "Because of me? Because we're seeing each other."

Angie reached out and covered his hand with hers, trying to reassure him. "No. It's a lot of things. And it's been happening for the last two years, so it's not just you, Jay. Although he did say some things that weren't exactly nice." She hadn't meant to tell him that last part, and didn't know why the words had even come out. And she wished she could take them back, because Jay stiffened slightly and pulled away, his eyes questioning as he stared at her for a few long seconds.

He finally let out another sigh and stretched out on the grass beside her, turning to his side and propping his head on one hand. He kept watching her, then finally patted the grass next to him.

Angie pushed the funnel cake away then laid back, her pose the mirror image of his. Only a few inches separated them. Jay looked down, then reached out and grabbed her hand. His thumb traced circles along the back of her knuckles and he didn't say anything for the longest time, just looked down at their joined hands.

"I'm sorry, I shouldn't have said anything."

"It's okay. And I can't say I'm surprised." He took a deep breath and looked up at her through partially-lowered lids. "Did you want to tell me what he said? You don't have to—"

"It wasn't anything specific, just things like to stay away from you because you weren't good enough for me. And that, well, that you were going to cause me heartache."

Jay nodded then looked back down at their hands. Angie wondered if he could hear the pounding of her heart in the silence between them, then wondered if she should say something to break the awful silence.

"Anything else?"

She thought about lying, just shaking her head and saying no. But Jay was watching her, his gaze steady and focused, almost as if he was waiting for her to lie. So she took a deep breath and looked down, deciding to tell him the truth.

"Just that you had a reputation for, um, getting around."

Jay's answering laughter was short and caustic, followed by muttered cursing. His fingers briefly tightened around hers before he broke the contact. But he didn't move away. Instead, he gently reached over and grabbed her chin, tilting her head up so she would look at him. His eyes were shadowed, filled with emotions ranging from regret and disappointment to worry and something else she couldn't read.

"Angie, I'm not going to lie to you and tell you I've been a saint, because I haven't. But I'm not as bad as everyone likes to believe I am. I, uh, haven't been known to settle down so people make more of it than they should."

Angie nodded, not knowing what else to say, or even if there was anything she could say. She knew going in that Jay wasn't a saint—far from it—but that hadn't meant anything to her then, not when she was just looking for some excitement.

And she hoped it didn't mean anything now. She kept reminding herself she wasn't looking for a relationship, wasn't planning on anything long term. At least, that's what she tried to do, from the very beginning. It wasn't Jay's fault that she found herself thinking of him more and more each day. It wasn't Jay's fault that she enjoyed spending time with him, even if it was just talking with him.

"Did Dave give you a reason for my, um, getting around?"

"No, of course not! And I didn't bother to ask because it's not my business. It's not his, either."

Jay laughed at her outrage then leaned forward and dropped a quick kiss on the tip of her nose. "Well, I happen to think it is, since we're seeing each other. And regardless of what everyone likes to think, I don't screw around if I'm dating someone. I was on the receiving end of that when I was married."

Angie leaned back, certain her mouth was open in shock. "You were married?"

""Yeah, about nine years ago, for an excruciating five months. It wasn't long after I got into the fire department." Jay paused, a small frown deepening the small lines of his forehead. "Dave didn't tell you that?"

"Uh, no." And neither did you, she thought. Did it make a difference?

Angie leaned back, her earlier shock slowly leaving, replaced by...she wasn't sure what. Jay had been married. Did it matter? Would she have still gone out with him? She closed her eyes for a brief second. No, it didn't matter. Not to her. And yes, she would have still gone out with him. His past didn't make a difference in how she felt—how she was starting to feel. Especially not something that had happened so long ago and lasted for such a short time.

She turned back to Jay, hoping he hadn't noticed

her slight pause, her surprise. "What happened?"

Jay studied her for a few seconds, his gray eyes a little too intense, a little too watchful. He finally grinned, a small half smile that just tugged at the corners of his mouth. "The whole thing was a mistake, we should have never gotten married in the first place. She didn't like me working night shift, didn't understand that was part of the job even though she already knew about it." He laughed, the sound sharp and empty of all humor before he looked away, his gaze now focused on the ground between them.

"She said she didn't like being home alone so she decided to use me working night shift as the perfect excuse to go out and party. And if I couldn't be there, well, there were plenty of other guys who would." He glanced up then looked away with a shrug. "I came home early one morning and found her in bed with someone else."

"Oh, Jay, I'm so sorry."

"Hey, don't be. It was a long time ago. It didn't even bother me then, which is how I knew we should've never been together in the first place." His smile was back in place, hesitant, not quite as bright. He reached out for her hand and squeezed. "So. Now that all my secrets are out, does any of it bother you?"

Angie leaned forward and pressed her mouth against his, increasing the pressure until his mouth opened under hers. She swept her tongue against his then pulled away before she lost control. "No. No, it doesn't bother me."

Jay smiled then rolled to his back, pulling her down so her head was resting on his chest. She brought her hand up and laid it next to her cheek, his skin warm beneath the shirt. She closed her eyes and sighed.

"I just wish Dave would get over it." She spoke the words softly and didn't realize that Jay had heard her until his arms tightened around her.

"Yeah. Me too."

Chapter Fifteen

Jay tightened his arms around Angie's waist, pulling her closer as he broke the kiss. Her eyes were partly closed, her lips full and wet from his kisses. A light flush caressed her cheeks, the light from the moon giving her skin an ethereal glow. Jay leaned forward and pressed his mouth to hers once more, unable to resist.

He didn't want to let her go.

He had to let her go.

They were standing in the small parking lot outside his apartment, next to her car. She had met him here earlier in the evening for their date.

Because he couldn't pick her up at her own house. Not when Dave was home.

He pulled away again and rested his forehead against hers. He wanted to ask her in but was afraid to. If he asked her in, he'd want her to spend the night—all night. He wanted more than the hurried encounters and stolen opportunities of the last few weeks that made him feel like they were sneaking around. He wanted to sleep with her in his arms and wake up to her smile in the morning instead of kissing her goodbye in the middle of the night before she left for home.

Tonight, he wanted her all night long. But he didn't ask, was too afraid to ask. Afraid she'd say no. And he wasn't foolish enough to expect her to say yes.

"I had fun tonight." Her voice was soft, her breath warm against his neck. He tightened his hold around her waist and smiled.

"I did, too."

Her hands moved up his sides and wrapped around his neck as she pressed her lips to his. But the kiss was over too quickly, giving his body just a sampling of the burn she could ignite inside him.

And right this minute, he wanted nothing more than for that burn to consume him. But it wasn't fair of him to create even more tension between her and Dave by acting on that desire, by asking her to spend the entire night with him—no matter how much he wanted it.

"I don't have to go home right now."

Her words echoed his desire so closely that he thought he imagined them. But her face was turned up to his, the barest hint of a smile teasing the corners of her lush mouth. And deep in her eyes was a hint of the same passion, the same need, that he felt himself.

"What about—"

She pressed her fingers against his mouth, silencing him as she shook her head. "I don't answer to anyone but myself, Jay."

Instead of freeing him, the words froze him to the spot. He wanted nothing more than to take her into his apartment, to feel her body against his, to lose himself deep inside her.

So why was he standing there like a brain-dead idiot?

Angie smiled up at him, and that full smile kicked his mind into gear. He reached up for her hand then turned, leading the way to his apartment. Neither of them spoke, not even after he had closed and locked the door. He went to move past her, thinking to play host and offer her something to drink, but she grabbed him and pressed against him, her mouth hot and insistent against his. They tore at each other's clothing, leaving a trail of shoes and shirts and pants along the hallway to his bedroom. Her bra landed somewhere near the edge of his bed, followed by his briefs until, finally, they were pressed against each other, bare flesh to bare flesh.

Jay moaned and stepped back, letting his eyes wander over her. From her full breasts, with their nipples puckered into tight peaks, begging for attention, to her taut abs, down past the flare of her rounded hips, to the long length of her toned and tanned legs.

He groaned again and reached out, cupping the full weight of her breast in one hand. His thumb grazed her nipple, feeling it tighten even more under his touch. He lowered his head and captured the peak in his mouth, sucking and nipping as he ran his other hand down along her side.

Another groan escaped him when her hand wrapped around his hard length, stroking him with hard, even strokes. He stepped back until the backs of his legs hit the edge of the bed, then toppled backward, pulling Angie down on top of him.

Their mouths crashed together, hungry and wet. He groaned again, needing to touch her, taste her. He wrapped his hands around her waist and pulled, dragging her up the length of his body until she straddled his face.

He looked up at her, saw her watching with glazed eyes, then raised his mouth to her. She gasped at the touch, then moaned when he ran his tongue along her clit. Back and forth, harder, dipping his tongue inside her.

She leaned back, her hands digging into his thighs as her hips thrust forward, opening to him even more. And he feasted, nipping and licking, his tongue delving inside her until he felt her begin to tighten. He wrapped an arm around her hips and held her against his mouth as her hips bucked. A low moan reached his ears, a wail of pleasure followed by the sound of his name being called in a hoarse cry of pleasure.

And he still didn't stop, just held her to him and tasted, feasted as if he was a dying man granted one last meal.

"Jay, please." The soft sound of her ragged plea shattered his willpower and he released her, giving her the freedom to roll to her side. Her breathing echoed around him and he slid to the side of the bed, his hand tearing at the nightstand drawer and groping blindly inside. His fingers closed over the box of condoms and he pulled one out, ripping it open and rolling it down his hard length before reaching her side.

He pulled her in his arms and kissed her, devouring her, his tongue thrusting in an imitation of what was yet to come.

Jay groaned then rolled to his back, pulling her with him and adjusting her hips over his. She broke the kiss and placed her palms flat on his chest, pushing herself up as she tilted her hips and lowered herself onto him.

"Angie, oh, God." He gritted his teeth and let his head drop back as she rode him, long, hard, slow. Sensation gripped him, clenching his gut, burning him from the inside out. He opened his eyes and looked up at her, at her parted lips and glazed eyes burning with the same desire that gripped him.

She brought her hands to her chest and grabbed her breasts, squeezing them together and pushing them up. A groan escaped him as he watched, mesmerized. She rolled each nipple between her fingers, squeezing, and he felt her body clench around his cock with an answering tremble.

Then she lowered her hand and reached between them, her finger gliding along her clit. His breathing tore at his chest in short gasps as he watched their joining. Angie pushed herself up, sliding up his length, then down, until his cock disappeared completely inside her. Again, up then down, the sensation exquisite, the torture unbearable.

He grabbed her with both hands, his fingers hard against the flesh of her hips, and moved her in his own rhythm, harder, faster. She cried out again as her body clenched around him, squeezing his cock, pushing him to the edge.

He dug his heels into the mattress and drove up into her, again.

Faster. Harder.

Again.

Once more.

He threw his head back and called her name, thrusting one final time before he exploded inside her. Lights danced along his eyelids, as red as the flames consuming him. Angie fell against him, her breath hot against his neck, her skin moist and warm against his chest.

He wrapped his arms around her and kissed her, deep, demanding, possessing. Minutes went by, languid and slow as his heart beat hard in his chest.

Angie lifted her head and stared down at him, a lazy smile on her flushed face. She leaned down for another kiss then eased off him, curling against his side with her head tucked against his shoulder.

He closed his eyes and gently ran his hand along her arm, struck by the feeling of contentment washing over him.

And wondered why it was so wrong of him to want *this*, with *this* woman, every night.

**

"Jay."

Angie pushed the hair from her face and nudged the hard body next to hers. He shifted and pulled her tighter against him as her fuzzy brain tried to remember why she was shaking him awake. She closed her eyes and snuggled closer to him, feeling the warmth of his body lulling her back into sleep.

Pounding, loud and insistent, teased the sliver of consciousness that hadn't yet succumbed to sleep. She mumbled and shifted, not wanting to get up, not wanting to move away from Jay's arms.

The pounding continued and Jay stirred next to her. His arms tightened around her and his lips trailed a warm path along the side of her neck. She leaned into him, a sleepy smile on her face as her body responded, wakening under his touch. He rolled over on top of her, his knee gently nudging her legs apart, his cock hard and ready between her thighs.

The pounding came again, sharp and loud.

"Dammit, I'm going to kill whoever that is."

Angie smiled against Jay's mouth, her body moving against his, already reaching for him. "Maybe they'll go away."

But there it came again, the loud banging. Jay swore and dropped his head to the pillow next to hers, then rolled away and climbed out of the bed.

"The damn building better be on fire, or I really am going to kill whoever's there."

She watched the play of muscles along his back and ass as he marched across the room, and smiled in sleepy appreciation. He tore open a dresser drawer and snagged a pair of gym shorts and pulled them on. He looked down and noticed his obvious erection, swore again, then stepped out of them and reached for a pair of jeans. Angie couldn't help it, she laughed.

He paused and turned to her, his brows raised in question. "Is something funny?"

"Not a thing."

He pulled on the zipper, wincing as he adjusted himself, then gave up before coming back to the bed. He leaned over her, giving her a nice view of his broad chest and tight abs. She ran a hand across his chest as he kissed her, hard and quick.

"Hold that thought." He squeezed her hip then walked out of the bedroom, swearing under his breath as the pounding resumed.

Angie sighed and closed her eyes, hoping that Jay wouldn't take too much time getting rid of whoever was at the door. She curled onto her side, snuggling into the warmth that still held a scent of Jay, and waited.

"Where the fuck is she?"

Angie's eyes shot open and her heart rose up into her throat. She froze, panicked, at the bellow that echoed through the apartment. She heard Jay's voice, pitched low, reasonable, but she couldn't make out the words through the buzzing in her ears.

"I said where the fuck is she? I know she's here, her car's out front!"

"Shit. Oh shit, oh shit, oh shit." Angie jumped from the bed then stumbled, her foot catching in the sheet. She untangled her leg and quickly looked around, searching for her clothes.

"Dave, stop. You need to calm down."

"Don't tell me to calm down. Where is my sister?"

Heavy footsteps started toward the bedroom then stopped. She heard a gasp, then the sound of pushing and more swearing.

Where in the hell were her clothes?

She tore through the mess scattered on the floor by the bed, finally finding her bra and underwear. Shit, where was her shirt? It had be here somewhere—

"Are those her pants? What the fuck, Moore! Angie, dammit, get out here."

Oh shit, oh shit, oh shit.

Her damn clothes were scattered in the hallway, just where they had dropped last night.

Probably right with Jay's clothes.

This wasn't good. This wasn't good at all.

Angie spun around the room, looking for

something, anything, to put on. Dave and Jay were arguing, and it sounded like Jay was trying to keep Dave from storming into the bedroom. But she knew her brother, knew he couldn't be stopped once he put his mind to something. And she was pretty sure he was in no mood to be stopped.

And why was even here? Why?

She pushed the question away. It didn't matter why he was here, just that he was. And if she didn't get out there and do something, something even worse was going to happen.

She had no idea what could actually be worse than this right now, but she knew there had to be something.

"Dave, man, c'mon, you need to leave. Now's not the time—"

"Get away from me Jay or I swear to God—"

"Dammit Dave, listen to me. We can have this out later but you can't go back there."

"Don't tell me what I can do. Angie! Dammit, I know you're here."

"Dave, I mean it, get out."

"Bullshit."

Angie heard something that sounded suspiciously like flesh hitting flesh and she made up her mind. Screw her clothes. She yanked the sheet off the bed and wrapped it around her then tore into the hall, afraid of what she would see.

And damned her imagination for being right.

Dave was pushing against Jay, trying to get by him as he blocked the hallway. Her brother's face was red with rage and he pushed Jay again, his hands clenched into fists.

Fear flared briefly in her gut at the sight. She had

never seen Dave this furious before, and she didn't know what he might do.

"Dammit Jay, get out of my way or I'll—"

"Stop! Just stop!" Angie's voice fell over them, stopping the shouting. Jay turned to look at her, worry and concern clear on his face. She met his gaze and shook her head the slightest bit, trying to tell him that it was okay, that she was fine.

Except the look on Dave's face told her things weren't going to be fine again for a long time. His brows lowered in an angry slash above his dark eyes and he glowered at her, his fury making her take a step back in shock. And then, before she even saw it coming, he reached out with both hands and grabbed Jay around the shoulders, pushing him into the wall with such force that a picture fell to the floor. Glass shattered, the sound barely heard above her brother's roar.

"Damn you! What the hell are you doing with my sister?" Dave pushed him again and Angie looked on in horror as one of his hands clenched into a fist aimed directly at Jay's chin.

But Jay didn't move, not to block her brother, not to push him away, not to hit him. Not even to defend himself. He just stood there, and Angie knew that if she didn't do something—now!—Jay was just going to take whatever Dave handed him.

She gripped the sheet with one hand and ran toward them, getting between them and pushing her brother back with a hand in the middle of his chest. "Dave, no! Stop!"

"Angie, get out of my way."

"Ang, please, just go back to the room."

She faced Jay, letting him know with one quick

look that she would do no such thing, then turned back to her brother. "Dave, stop, please. Just go home."

"Angie, get out of my way."

"Dave, we can talk about this—" But she didn't get to finish because Dave grabbed her arm and pulled her away from Jay, then pushed her to the side. Her feet tangled in the trailing end of the sheet and she stumbled before regaining her balance.

"You fucking asshole! Don't you dare touch her!" Jay suddenly stood between her and Dave, his right arm held behind him, keeping her safely behind his back.

"Me? You're the one who needs to stay off of her! Do you hear me?"

Jay stepped closer, his voice pitched low and dangerous. "Get the hell out of my house. Now."

"Fine. Angie, let's go."

She looked up to find Dave watching her, fury still burning in his eyes, his face still flushed with anger. And she shook her head, just a small movement, because she was afraid to speak, afraid her words would come out on a choke.

Afraid, for just a second, of the man she called brother.

The ensuing silence was deafening, so oppressive that nobody moved. Angie kept her eyes glued to her brother's face, expecting another explosion, but what she saw was worse.

It was like all the life just drained from him in one breath. His shoulders sagged and the fury left his eyes in the space of one blink. And in their place was a despair so sharp that she felt the breath catch in her throat at the sight.

And then everything she saw was gone, replaced with a cool mask of indifference so quickly, she wondered if she had imagined seeing it in the first place. Dave's eyes never left hers as he shook his head and took a step back. Then he turned and left, slamming the door behind him.

She remained frozen for another long second before emotion crashed over her, battering her. She gulped in a deep breath, trying to breathe, trying to get her heart to stop pounding so quickly.

"Oh God, I am so sorry. I'm sorry. I can't...I'll get my things and..." Her voice trailed off and she turned away from Jay, unable to meet his gaze, then walked back toward the bedroom. She stopped to pick up the clothes as she went, balling them and holding them against her chest.

"Angie, stop. Come here." Jay stepped around her and pulled the clothes from her hands then dropped them to the floor. He wrapped his arms around her and pulled her close, guiding her head to his shoulder before rubbing one hand up and down her back.

"I'm sorry. I'm so sorry."

"Shh, stop. It's not your fault, so stop, okay?" His whisper was soft in her ear, his voice low and soothing. Minutes went by before she finally stopped holding herself so rigidly, finally allowed herself to be comforted. She wrapped her arms around his waist and held on tight, afraid to let go, afraid of what had just happened.

Angie closed her eyes, squeezing them tight against the building tears. She needed to leave, knew she should just get dressed and go home, but she couldn't bring herself to move, not just yet.

Not when she felt so safe in Jay's arms.

"You okay?"

"Yeah. I mean, I guess. Yeah, I'll be fine." Her voice shook, cracking on the last word. Fine? She didn't know if she'd ever be fine again, not after seeing a side to her brother she didn't know existed.

"You don't sound too sure about that."

Angie pulled away from Jay and tried to smile. "I'll be fine, honest."

He studied her, doubt clear in his gray eyes, but didn't question her. Instead he lowered his mouth to hers, the kiss comforting, reassuring. "Why don't you jump in the shower while I fix breakfast?"

Angie shook her head. "Thanks, but I should probably go home."

"Not yet, okay? Give him some time to cool off. Knowing Dave, that might take a while. Okay?"

Angie chewed on her lower lip, not sure what to do, even though she knew Jay was right. She finally nodded and received a small smile back as answer, then moved into the bedroom. But she made it only as far as the bed, where she sat down and stared into nothing.

Jay was right, and not only in what he said. Because hidden under his words, in a tone that even Angie could hear, was the worry that Dave needed more than cooling off. Worry that his anger had been way over the line, extreme even for a protective older brother.

And that scared her more than anything.

Chapter Sixteen

A muffled roar sounded overhead, a hungry rumbling that grew louder with each passing second. Heat banked from the ceiling, down to the floor and through the layers of protective gear.

The beast was hungry, feeding.

Sweat rolled between his shoulder blades and down his chest, morphing into steam that simmered against his flesh. Jay dragged the hose line forward, grunting when it snagged on something behind him. He turned in the smoky darkness and yanked, then moved further into the room on his knees.

Mikey came up behind him, shouting something, her voice muffled and unintelligible behind the mask. He shook his head and gave her a curt wave, then aimed the nozzle toward the beast and opened it.

Water sprayed out in a hard stream, attacking the growing flames with a roar of its own. Steam filled the room, blanketing them in moist heat. He dropped to his stomach and ignored the singeing of his ears and neck, never losing sight of his aim.

Something pushed against his shoulder, hard, and he turned. Mikey was pointing up and he looked behind her, swore as he rolled to his back and aimed the nozzle against the flames dancing across the ceiling above them.

Another roar erupted from somewhere deep inside the building, followed by a loud crash. The sound was muted in the smoke and flame, the quality distorted, haunting. Jay clenched his teeth against the building heat and moved the nozzle back and forth, not willing to let the beast win.

The radio crackled next to his ear, echoing the noise from Mike's radio beside him. Shouted orders pierced the roar, telling everyone to pull back.

"Son of a bitch!" Jay shouted, knowing that only Mike might be able to hear him. He pushed up to his knees and kept the water aimed in front of him, knocking back the growing wall of flames as they backed out of the room.

Groaning came from somewhere above them and they both stopped their retreat, looking up through smoke and flame. The sound grew louder, ripping and twisting, the noise mutated by the dense smoke growing thicker around them.

He looked over at Mike and their eyes locked for a brief second before they both dove out of the hallway and down the staircase, each holding the other, pulling, pushing, shoving. The ceiling above them crashed down in a shower of drywall and timber and scorching heat, a pile of burning debris landing where they had been a second before.

"Fuck!" Something crashed hard against Jay's ankle and he kicked it off as scorching heat seared his skin. But they kept moving down the stairwell, following the hose line down and out until daylight greeted them.

Hands grabbed them, pulling them away from the building. Jay brushed them away and stood as he yanked his face mask off, taking deep breaths of the warm summer air.

"Son of a bitch!" He gasped, still filling his lungs. He turned to look at Mikey, to make sure she was okay.

Their eyes met and they both broke into smiles then high-fived each other.

"Saved your ass again. Next round's on you."

"Bullshit. I saved your ass again, next round's on you!" Jay laughed then took a step forward. Pain shot through his ankle, sharp and biting, causing his breath to hiss. He grimaced then tried to shake it off but he wasn't fast enough. Mikey was suddenly by his side, her hand gripping his shoulder.

"What is it?"

"Nothing, probably just a burn. Something caught my leg when we were face-planting the staircase." He took another step, gingerly testing his weight on his ankle, then took another. Mikey swore then grabbed his arm and dragged it over her shoulder, supporting his weight.

He grimaced but didn't say anything, knowing he'd need her help for at least a few more feet until he could reach the engine. He'd be fine as soon as he could get out of his gear.

They walked toward the engine, Mike helping him step over the various hose lines until they reached the back step. Jay shrugged out of his breathing apparatus then unclipped his coat and dropped it next to the bottle. He undid the clip and

Velcro closure of his pants, pulled the suspenders down his arms, then shoved the pants down and pulled his foot from the boot.

There was a dark scorch mark near the bottom hem of the right leg, and he winced when he saw it. He sat on the back step and pulled his other foot out then yanked up the leg of his uniform pants.

"Damn, that's going to leave a mark." Mikey whistled and bent over his leg, gently pulling at his sock. Jay tried not to wince as she pulled the damp material from his foot but she noticed anyway.

The outside of his leg, just above his right ankle, was red and blistered, the skin stretched tight and already throbbing. He breathed in through his teeth and gently rotated his foot, wincing again.

"It'll be fine."

"Yeah, right." Mikey dropped her gear next to his. "I'll go get Dave."

"Mike, no. I'll be fine, seriously."

"Let her get Dave."

Jay turned to see Pete standing next to them, eyeing his burned leg with detachment. He wanted to object, wanted to tell them both he was fine, that he would just walk it off. But the stinging throbbing wasn't going away, and he knew neither of them would buy it.

Jay let out a deep breath and shook his head, knowing he wasn't going to win this one. For an officer, Pete was pretty laid back—except on the fire ground. And his expression told Jay loud and clear that he wasn't going to talk his way out of this one, no matter how much he might want to. Jay sighed again and fixed Mike with a steady gaze, his expression serious. "Get Jimmy instead."

Mike nodded then walked away, not saying anything. He hadn't expected her to, not since he had already told her what had happened the other morning. Well, the abbreviated version, anyway.

Jay shifted, turning so he could raise his leg and stretch it out in front of him along the back step. The diamond plate was cold and rough under his skin but he didn't care. He closed his eyes, blocking out the low rumble of the diesel engine, the squelch of radios and shouts from the fire ground. The scene around him was loud, chaotic, busy—and didn't faze him in the least.

The discomfort in his ankle faded into dullness and Jay felt himself dozing off, a slight separation from the world around him. A searing pain shot through his leg and he bolted upright. His eyes shot open and he leaned forward, trying to grab his leg, only to have his hands pushed away.

"Son of a bitch!" He hissed the words through clenched teeth and glared at Dave. The man gave him a steely look then turned away, studying his ankle. He twisted his leg to get a closer look at the burn, and didn't bother being gentle about it. His gloved fingers pushed around the mottled blistering skin, moving around and outward from the burn.

Jay clenched his jaw and looked over at Mike, who was watching with an expression of apology on her face.

Dave reached behind him and grabbed some gauze and ointment from the medic box, then fixed Jay with another hard stare.

"Looks like it's at least sprained. This might hurt." Then he proceeded to slap burn ointment on his ankle with such pressure that Jay felt his stomach clench with pain and nausea.

"Fucking shit! Dammit, that's enough. It's fine!" He finally pulled his leg from Dave's grip and shot him a hard look, not surprised to see an answering glare on the man's face.

"What the hell, Dave? Really?" Mike stepped closer, ready to pull Dave away. But the man straightened and threw the roll of gauze at her, his anger obvious.

"Then you do it. Bring him to the medic when you're done." He stormed away, leaving surprised silence behind him.

"What the hell was that all about?" Pete stared at after Dave, his brows lowered in a frown. Jay glanced at Mike and shook his head, telling her not to say anything. She shot him a dirty look, letting him know that she hadn't planned on it.

"Guess he's just in a bad mood."

"You think?" Pete turned back and studied him, watching. "Well, you heard him. Can you make it over to the medic?"

"Pete, I'm fine. I don't need to go to the hospital. Just wrap the damn thing so I can get back to work."

Pete and Mike stared at him before they both started laughing. He shot Mike a dirty look then grabbed the gauze from her hand, intending to wrap the ankle himself. Except when he bent over to do it, he realized why they had both started laughing.

In the short time since he had come outside, the blister had swollen and grown bigger, pulling against the shiny red skin surrounding it. And beneath the blister, his foot had started swelling, almost twice its normal size. There was no way in hell he was getting his boots back on, let alone getting back to work.

He shot Mike another dirty look then threw the gauze at her, ignoring her laugh as she fumbled and almost dropped it. He closed his eyes and leaned his head against the engine in frustration.

"Son of a bitch."

Chapter Seventeen

Music from the jukebox filled the bar with the fast beat of a rocking country song. The crack of pool balls banging against each other echoed in the corner, followed by laughter and joking.

Angie looked up from the cooler and glanced over at the small crowd, a frown on her face.

Not everyone was laughing and joking.

She twisted the top from the bottle then pushed it across the bar toward Jay. He smiled his thanks but it was nothing more than a flat lifting of his lips as he lifted the bottle to his mouth and took a long swallow. He didn't bother to move from the barstool, where he had been perched for the last hour.

Angie glanced at the crutches propped next to him, then back over to the crowd in the corner where Jay's coworkers were gathered. Several of them were shooting pool, ribbing each other with each shot. A few others were huddled around one table, talking and joking.

Everyone except her brother.

Dave sat a few feet away, apart from everyone else, his chair tipped back against the wall. The expression on his face was blank, unreadable.

She didn't need to worry about other customers, because it was midweek and a slow night. There were less than a handful of people besides Jay's crew, and everyone was taken care of.

She wished it was crowded, that the room was teeming with people and noise and music and bustle. That would be so much better than now. The underlying tension was so thick, Angie could feel it from her place behind the bar. She sighed and pushed her hair behind her ears then leaned against the counter, her mind still whirling.

She hated the tension, hated the rift between Jay and Dave. Hated that she was the cause of it. But she had no idea what to do to make things right. Worse, she was afraid things would only deteriorate even more.

And that didn't even count the tension at home. She and Dave had barely spoken since the morning he had shown up at Jay's. No, that wasn't right. The tension had been brewing before then, the silence and strain finally coming to an explosive head that morning. And the tension was starting to wear on her, making her tired and edgy and miserable. Not just at him, but at work. And school. And here.

She sighed again and looked over at Jay, her guilt increasing as she watched him stare into the bottle, his mind elsewhere. Was the tension she was picking up on just between him and Dave? Or was it between him and the entire shift? She didn't think she could handle being responsible for that as well. The rift between Jay and her brother was bad enough.

"How's the ankle?"

"Fine."

"When are they going to let you go back to work?"

Jay shrugged and took another swallow of beer. "Next trick. I hope."

Angie nodded then toyed with the damp rag in her hand, needing something to do with her hands. She felt bad for thinking it, but she was glad he had the extra time off because they had spent much of it together.

Which somehow made her feel even guiltier. How wrong was it that she could enjoy spending time with him, when it was so obviously making things worse for him at work? And worse for her at home.

She glanced back over again at her brother and saw him watching them with a scowl on his face. One of the guys pushed against his arm and Dave turned away, leaning over to listen to whatever was being said. He shrugged then went back to leaning against the wall, his head tilted back and his eyes closed.

Angie sighed again.

"You don't have to keep me company, you know. You can go over and hang with them, I won't mind." And she didn't mind. She really didn't. She wanted Jay to go hang with his friends, wanted this tension she felt smothering everything around her to disappear.

"No, I'm good."

"Jay." She paused, trying to figure out what she wanted to say. No—how she wanted to say it. And she couldn't understand why she suddenly felt so uncomfortable, so unsure.

Jay was watching her, waiting for her to continue,

a small frown creasing his face. That was another thing that bothered her: he seemed to be frowning more, instead of smiling that boyish half-smile that sent shivers of excitement racing through her. She leaned forward and placed her hand on his arm, squeezing gently. "You need to go hang with everyone. I can't handle all this tension, can't stand feeling like it's all because of me."

"Angie, stop worrying, there's no tension, okay?"

"Really? How can you say that? Just look!" She waved her hand, motioning between him and the corner, encompassing everything in-between. Jay snagged her hand mid-air and curled his fingers around hers before leaning down and kissing her knuckles.

"Angie, everything at work is fine, and the only tension is between me and Dave."

"And that's my fault."

"No, it's not. That all falls on Dave, okay? He'll eventually get over it."

"And if he doesn't?"

"Then that's on him as well." He leaned across the bar and brushed his lips against hers in a quick kiss that was no less heated for its brevity. He pulled back and offered a small smile, a real smile, and squeezed her hand. "If I go over there, will you stop worrying?"

She smiled back and nodded, but didn't say anything because anything she said would be a lie. She was going to worry, regardless. Because no matter what he said, this *was* her fault, all of it. If she hadn't thrown herself at him that one night, nothing else would have happened, of that she was sure.

Jay would have never asked her out, would have

never let the thought cross his mind. Because he was Dave's friend, and she was his friend's sister.

And even she knew the crude saying about friends coming before women. Especially when it was your friend's sister.

Jay squeezed her hand again then slid off the barstool, ignoring his crutches as he limped over to the pool table. She watched him lean over and say something to Pete, heard the laughter that followed. He grabbed a pool stick from the rack along the wall and joined the game, but not before glancing back at her with a smile and a wink.

She smiled back then turned to look at Dave, saw that he hadn't moved positions, that he was still glowering at Jay. A few seconds went by before he turned his head and looked in her direction. The scowl didn't leave his face. If anything, he frowned even more. His phone must have beeped or vibrated or something, because he looked away long enough to glance at the screen. And the frown deepened, his face turning red as he tossed the phone on the table and ignored it. Like he was ignoring her.

Angie sighed and started wiping down the clean bar, her thoughts running in dizzying circles.

Maybe Jay had been right, maybe the tension was only between Dave and him. That didn't ease her guilt, because she was still responsible for it.

Just like she was the one responsible for the tension between Dave and her. Nobody else, just her.

Yeah, friends were supposed to come before women. But what about that other saying? The one that said family came first? Dave was the only family she had left, so what did that say about her?

**

Angie shut the door behind her, trying to be quiet. The living room light was on, but that didn't mean Dave was awake.

She really hoped he wasn't awake because she wasn't in the mood to deal with him tonight. She was tired, so tired and drained. If he saw her dragging herself in like this, there would be another confrontation and he'd demand that she quit the bar. Again.

That was if he even bothered saying anything to her at all. Lately he had just been giving her the silent treatment. Silent—except for his eyes. They were filled with either disappointment or disapproval, and she wasn't sure which bothered her more.

Yes, she did. Disappointment. Seeing that hurt her more than she wanted to admit, and she didn't know what to do about it.

She didn't know if there was anything she could do about it.

Her mouth opened in a long yawn that she didn't bother to stifle as she moved through the living room. Steps sounded to her left and she looked over, surprised to see Dave walking out of the kitchen.

"I didn't expect you home."

Angie flinched at the accusation and lifted her chin. "It is my home, you know."

"No, I wouldn't, considering how little you're actually here anymore."

"Dave, I'm tired. Can we please not do this right now?"

"Do what?"

"This. Argue. The tension and the guilt. All of it. Can we please just not do it?"

He stepped into the living room and sat back on

the sofa, leaning back as he watched her with one raised brow. "I'm not arguing. And if you're feeling guilty about something, well, I'm not sure what I have to do about that."

"You have everything to do with it!" She leaned against the stair railing and folded her arms across her chest. "The way you've been acting, the stunt you pulled the other week showing up at Jay's. Even tonight, how you were acting, staring everyone down. Why? I don't understand!"

"You don't understand?"

"No, Dave, I don't. You keep treating me like I'm twelve years old. And how you're treating Jay. He's your friend!"

"No, he was my friend."

Angie swallowed against the thickness in her throat and shook her head. "Why? Because we're seeing each other? Why does that make a difference?"

"Because it does, Angie."

"God, this is so stupid. I don't understand, I really don't. Why is it so wrong for me to like someone you work with? Why is it so wrong for me to be having fun and enjoying myself?"

"You won't be saying that when he breaks your heart. Trust me, I know Jay. And if you think for one minute that he's somebody you can trust, then you're fooling yourself."

"Oh my God, I can't believe we're having this discussion! Do you even realize that we've been dating for close to three months already?" Angie took a deep breath and wiped her hand across her eyes. "And so what if it doesn't work out? Don't you think I realize that's a possibility? Why does it matter when we just enjoy being together for now?"

"Because if either one of you had any respect for the boundaries, neither one of you would be seeing the other, that's why. And for that, I blame Jay."

"Well here's a newsflash for you, big brother. I'm the one who asked Jay out, not the other way around. And I asked him several times because he kept saying no, even after I threw myself at him! But he kept saying no. Because you were his friend. So don't blame Jay, blame me!"

Angie snapped her mouth closed, surprised at the anger lacing her voice. Dave's head snapped back as if he had been slapped, his brows drawn together in a scowl of anger and disappointment. Silence stretched around them, so heavy she felt herself smothering under its weight.

Dave finally stood, his expression still ominous as he approached her. He stopped next to her and looked down, disappointment clear in his dark eyes.

"I had more faith in you, Angela. But I guess I was wrong. So congratulations, I hope having your fun is worth destroying a friendship. And the relationship with your brother."

He pushed past her as she sagged against the railing, the finality in his words leaving her more stunned than any physical blow. Her chest heaved as her breath caught in her throat, her lungs tight with the effort to draw breath.

How could he even say such a thing to her? To accuse her of such things? She waited for anger to course through her body, waited for indignation and fury to overtake the tears that hovered at the corners of her eyes.

But all she felt was disappointment. And a keen sense of loss, as if something had been savagely ripped from her chest.

Because his accusations so closely resembled what she had been thinking earlier that evening. If she hadn't pursued Jay, none of this would have happened.

None of it.

Dave and Jay would still be friends.

Her family would still be intact and she and Dave wouldn't be strangers living under the same roof.

And she wouldn't be becoming attached to someone she had no right to be attached to.

Angie dropped to the bottom step and hugged her knees to her chest, rocking back and forth. Tears seeped from her closed eyes but she ignored them, her mind reeling and her heart breaking. Dave was right. About everything. If she hadn't pushed, none of this would be happening right now. So what if she'd had a crush on Jay? She'd had other crushes and never acted on them. That was part of life. So why had she pursued Jay? Why had she pushed it this one time? Was it because of the allure of having something—someone—who was off-limits?

None of this would be happening right now if not for her. If she hadn't thrown herself at Jay, hadn't kept pushing when he turned her down, life would be normal. No stress, no anger, no tension. She'd have her brother back. Her big brother, her only real family, the one constant in her life. The big brother who had looked out for her growing up, who made sure she was safe and happy. Who made sure she'd be able to pursue her dream career, who supported her and worried about her.

Dave was right. All of it was her fault.

She needed to think, needed to decide what to

do.

And wondered if she had the strength and courage to do the right thing.

Chapter Eighteen

Jay tossed the towel over the shower rod and grabbed his pants, pulling them on and working the zipper as he walked out of the bathroom. A quick glance at the clock told him that it was too early for Angie to be here, and he wondered who else would be knocking at the door.

Or maybe Angie was early.

He felt a grin tilt the corners of his mouth and decided not to mess with the button of his jeans. Of course, he'd feel like an ass if it wasn't Angie, but still.

He pulled the door open and his grin turned into a full smile when he saw Angie standing there. Her eyes dropped to his bare chest then lower, and he felt a moment of uncharacteristic ego and pride that just looking at him could bring a flush to her face.

Of course, he wasn't immune to her gaze, and felt some of the blood rush south as she looked him over.

He didn't say anything, just grabbed her hand and pulled her inside and against him for a long heated kiss. His cock was fully at attention now and he wondered if he could talk her into going to dinner late.

Considering she was early and all.

A second went by before he realized she wasn't pressing herself against him like he was used to, that she was actually pulling away instead. He released his hold on her and let her step back, studying her face.

Dark circles blemished the fragile skin under her eyes and her face was paler than normal. The corners of her mouth were turned down in something not quite a frown. The first inkling that something wasn't right went through him, twisting in his gut. He reached for her hand and led her to the sofa. He sat down next to her, turning so they were facing each other.

"What's wrong?"

"Jay, I..." Her voice drifted off and she looked away, her teeth pulling on her lower lip. She shook her head then took a deep breath, her hair falling forward and hiding her face.

He felt his stomach twist even further and he swallowed, wondering what was going on but afraid to hear, afraid that he already knew. He reached out and pushed the hair back behind her ear, his fingers lingering in the soft strands before he moved his hand away.

"Talk to me Angie. What is it?"

She finally looked up at him. The sheen of moisture in her eyes hit him in the gut, knocking the breath from his lungs. He clenched his jaw against the sensation and didn't move, afraid to breathe, afraid of what he saw in her eyes.

"Jay, I can't do this anymore. I'm sorry."

The reality was worse than he had imagined. A slice of something sharp and hard tore through his chest but he refused to acknowledge it, refused to give into it. He leaned back and watched her, saw the anguish in her dark brown eyes. He swallowed and shook his head, still not understanding.

Not wanting to understand.

"Do what, Angie? What is it you can't do anymore?"

"This. Us. Everything. I—I just can't, I'm sorry."

Jay was silent for a long time, watching her, praying that this was some kind of twisted joke. He wanted to rewind the last ten minutes and pretend he had never heard the knock on the door. Rewind the last twenty minutes so he could slip in the shower and knock himself unconscious.

Because anything would be better than this. Better than the desolation in her eyes, better than the gut-twisting agony that threatened to double him over in pain. He breathed in through his nose, deep, and held it, trying to settle the rampage of emotions destroying him. But it didn't help. He didn't know if anything would help.

Jay let out the breath and still said nothing, not sure if he could trust his voice to stay calm and level. Another minute went by and he knew he had to speak, had to ask.

"Why?"

Angie shook her head and looked away. He thought there should be some comfort in the turmoil she was so obviously feeling. If there was, he couldn't find it.

"It's...everything. The stress and the tension. The way things are between you and Dave. The way things are at home. I can't do it anymore, I can't. It's not worth it anymore."

A flash of anger burst inside him at her words. "Not worth it? Don't you think maybe I should have a say in if it's worth it or not? Or do you mean it's not worth it to you?"

"No. No, that's not what I meant. Don't you see? I'm the one responsible for all of it. And none of it would have happened if I hadn't chased after you. Even you said—"

"Angie, I don't care about that. Any of it. I care about you. Can you really sit there and say it's not worth it?"

Her mouth opened then closed again and she said nothing. She watched him with sad, moist eyes then shook her head. "I can't do it anymore, Jay. I'm sorry."

He clenched his jaw and looked away, not knowing what to say. The past few months with Angie had been the longest he had been with anyone for too many years to remember. And he had thought—well, it didn't matter what he thought, not anymore. Unless...

He looked back over at her, trying to reign in the avalanche of emotions that threatened to crush him. "Is there someone else?"

"What? No. God, no." She leaned forward and reached out with one trembling hand and cupped his cheek. Her touched seared his flesh and he nearly pulled away. But he couldn't, he didn't want to. Because damn him, he still wanted her touch. She was destroying something inside him and he still wanted her touch.

"There's nobody else, Jay."

He reached up and covered her hand with his, not knowing what else to say. And no matter what she said, he knew deep down that there was someone else.

Her brother. And her insanely misplaced loyalty to him—and to Jay's old friendship with him. But he didn't know what else to say, didn't know how to tell her that none of that mattered. He didn't know how to convince her that everything would work out regardless.

He only knew that something was shattering deep inside him, tearing him apart, and he didn't know what to do about it.

And still he didn't move, didn't say anything. Just watched her, watched the pain and tears in her eyes. And then he leaned forward, just the barest of movements, until his mouth was suddenly on hers. Soft, tender, hesitant.

He waited, expecting her to push him away. But she softened and pressed her body more tightly against his, a small moan escaping her as she wrapped her arms around his neck and surrendered to him.

He knew he should stop, knew that this could only make things worse. But he didn't. He wanted Angie one last time, wanted to make sure she would never forget him, that he would forever be emblazoned in her memory.

He ran his tongue along the closed seal of her lips, groaned when she opened for him and met his tongue with hers. Flames kissed his flesh wherever her hands roamed, along his shoulders and chest, down across his stomach.

To the zipper of his jeans.

Jay shifted as she pulled the zipper down,

reached in and grabbed him. He groaned at her touch, pressed himself more fully into her hand. She broke the kiss and pulled back, releasing him. But she didn't stand, didn't leave. Instead, she reached for the hem of her shirt and pulled it over head, tossing it to the floor. Her arms reached behind her, unclasping the bra, and the bright lacy material slid down her arms.

He reached out and traced her collarbone with one finger, surprised to see that his hand was trembling. Her head tilted back as he ran his finger down to her breast, tracing its fullness, moving closer to trace the outline of her nipple.

Her hand reached up and closed around his wrist, stopping him. Now she would leave. She would realize what they were doing was wrong, that she didn't want this.

But she didn't leave. She slid off the sofa and undid the snap of her linen capris. Her thumbs hooked into the waistband and she pushed them down past her hips, let them slide to her feet until she stood before him, wondrously bare to his eyes.

Jay's eyes caressed her body, memorizing each curve and indentation, memorizing how the curl of her hair rested over her shoulder and fell against one breast, how her chest rose and fell with each ragged breath and how her body flushed pink under his gaze.

He stood up and pulled her into his arms, claiming her mouth once more, wanting to possess her but knowing he could do no more than taste her this one last time. Then he bent over and wrapped one arm behind her legs and lifted her, carrying her into the bedroom and placing her gently in the middle of the bed.

He pushed his jeans down and kicked them

away, then stretched out beside her. Angie's eyes glistened with moisture and he leaned down, kissing each lid with infinite tenderness.

He heard her gasp, felt her chest heave under his, but he didn't stop. He placed light kisses along her face, behind her ear, down her throat.

And when she reached up to wrap her arms around his neck, he pushed her away, gently. Long enough to grab a condom from the nightstand and sheath himself. He rolled back over and stretched against her, on top of her, settling his weight between her legs. He braced his weight on his elbows and cupped her face in his hands, his eyes searching hers before he lowered his head and claimed her mouth in a searing kiss.

And drove himself deep inside her.

She gasped, her breath mingling with his, then raised her legs and wrapped them high around his waist. Her hips thrust against him, seeking, demanding.

But not yet. Not now.

He set the pace, slow, agonizingly slow. He pulled out, then eased back in, over and over, until the sheen of exertion covered both their bodies, until his breathing was as ragged and desperate as Angie's.

And then he felt it, a tight clench around his cock that pulled him even deeper, that threatened to bring him to his knees. Angie's head dropped back, her mouth parted as short gasps turned into moans of need. Her hips thrust, faster, searching, and Jay pulled back, almost pulled out of her, nearly killing himself with the torture.

"Angie, look at me." His voice was harsh, hoarse, ripped from a throat aching with raw emotion.

She shook her head, one tear falling from the corner of her eye.

"Angie, look at me." He begged. He didn't care, he wanted this—needed this—too much to care.

And then she opened her eyes, glazed with passion, filled with emotion. He held her head between his hands and thrust into her, harder, faster.

Deeper.

Demanding.

"Don't ever forget me, Angie."

Her body tightened around his, drawing him in, holding him, caressing him until she exploded around him. And still he wouldn't let her look away, needed to watch her as he found his own release inside her.

She finally turned her head to the side, breaking the contact that joined them together as much as their bodies had been joined. Jay released his breath and lowered himself against her, felt her arms coming up to hold him, her hands stroking his back in small circles.

He didn't know how much time had passed, seconds or minutes, but she stopped touching him and let her arms drop to the side. Coldness settled over him, reaching deep inside and filling him with a chill he didn't think would ever leave him.

He rolled off her, onto his back, and draped one arm over his eyes. He didn't want to see her now, didn't want anything to replace the last image he had of her in his mind.

The bed dipped as she climbed out, not saying anything. Her soft steps crossed the room, moved into the hall. He could hear her gathering her things, getting dressed and straightening up.

Then he heard the door open, the soft click as it

closed behind her.
    Angie was gone.

Chapter Nineteen

The words blurred in front of Jay and he blinked, trying to bring them back into focus. He didn't know why he bothered, though, because he had been reading the same article over and over and couldn't even guess at what it was about.

Reading. Yeah.

He wasn't reading, he was staring into nothing, hoping a numbness would somehow claim him. It hadn't happened in the past three days, why did he think it would happen now?

And the only reason he was still reading the paper—still holding it in front of him—was because he didn't feel like talking. To anyone. And if he got rid of the paper, he'd be expected to join in the conversation.

And that was the last thing he wanted.

Words and phrases drifted into his consciousness and he tried to push them away, tried to ignore the carrying on around him. But it was getting harder to do, harder to pretend that it didn't piss him off.

Because Dave and Jimmy were at the next table, carrying on with Pete and Adam, talking about Dave's sudden mood change.

And laughing about it. The fuckers.

Jay shifted in the hard chair and looked over, clenched his jaw then looked back down at the paper. He felt Mike studying him and he shot her a quick look, catching the question in her eye. Jay shook his head and said nothing.

What could he say?

"Well, whatever the hell it was, I'm glad you snapped out of it. You were becoming a miserable son of a bitch."

Dave laughed, the sound grating on Jay's nerves. "Yeah, I guess. But hey, at least I'm over it, and all is right in the world."

Jay couldn't handle it anymore, not without exploding and doing something he shouldn't. He tossed the paper on the table then stood up, his angry strides eating up the distance until he pushed through the door hard enough that it banged against the wall.

He wanted to hit something, *needed* to hit something. And if he didn't leave, that something would be Dave's smug face.

He turned toward the basement and took the stairs leading down at a jog, hitting the light switch as he turned the corner. He unbuttoned his uniform shirt and threw it over a hook then grabbed a pair of gloves from the shelf.

He didn't worry about lacing them, didn't care about anything except the bag hanging in front of him, daring him. He closed his eyes and took a deep breath, then stepped in close and jabbed. Once, twice.

Over and over, until the bag spun crazily under

his assault. And still he didn't stop, just kept pounding it, over and over, until sweat poured down his forehead and stung his eyes.

He tilted his head and wiped his face against his shoulder, then hit the bag again, his aim steady.

Jab. Thwack.

Jab. Thump.

Jab. Jab. Jab.

He stopped, his chest heaving, and rested his forehead against the bag. Dammit. Damn everything.

"Hey, Jay. Mind if we talk?"

Jay stiffened, not believing his ears, knowing he must be imagining things. He turned and blinked the sweat from his eyes, but the image in front of him didn't disappear.

"I have nothing to say to you."

Dave stepped closer, holding one hand out. Jay ignored him and ripped the gloves from his hands, then tossed them back on the shelf. He moved over to the weight bench, intent on ignoring him, but Dave followed, coming closer.

"Listen, I just wanted to apologize for acting like an ass. No hard feelings, right?"

Jay looked down, saw Dave extending his arm. For a handshake? Was he fucking serious?

He stepped back, knowing that he was dangerously close to using Dave as a punching bag, and shook his head.

"Fuck you."

Dave's hand dropped to his side and a look of surprise crossed his face at the cold words. He frowned, studying Jay, not saying anything for a few seconds.

"I'm trying to say I'm sorry, Jay. I don't want this

to come between our friendship."

"What? Are you fucking kidding me? You worry about that now? Now?" Jay snapped his mouth closed and took a step back, trying to put distance between them before he really did do something he'd regret.

"I'm not sure what you want me to say."

"How about nothing, okay? You son of a bitch. Where do you come off, coming down here and acting like everything's fine? Like I'm going to forget what you did?"

"What I did? Tell me Jay, what did I do?"

"You went overboard. You want to be pissed we were seeing each other? Fine. I get that. But you went overboard. You treated me like shit, and you put Angie through hell. Well congratulations, you got what you wanted. Now get the hell out of my sight."

"What the hell did you want me to do? You were screwing my little sister! I did what I had to do to protect her!"

Jay ran forward, intent on letting Dave have it, but stopped himself at the last minute. He held his clenched fists down at his side as he struggled to pull deep gulps of air into his lungs.

"I wasn't *screwing* her."

"Don't fucking lie, Jay. I know what I saw that morning, and you're not going to tell me you weren't screwing her."

"Hey, asshole, I wasn't screwing her." Jay repeated, his voice getting louder. "Did you ever to stop to think that maybe, just maybe, I care about her? No, of course you didn't, because you're the only one who matters."

"Bullshit Jay. I've known you for too long, I know how you are. So yeah, I did what I had to."

"What *you* had to do? Seriously? How? By making her miserable? By making her feel guilty? By making her choose between what she wants and what you want? Then congratulations, you just showed her how important she really is to you."

"Where the hell do you get off talking to me like that?"

"I'll talk to you however I want. Now get. The fuck. Out."

"Hey!"

The sharp word shattered the echo of their shouts and Jay stepped back, surprised to realize he was nearly nose to nose with Dave. He shook his head and walked back to the weight bench, not bothering to look at Mike as she stepped between them.

"Unless you two want everyone in the station to know what the hell is going on, both of you need to shut the hell up."

"Mike, this doesn't concern you."

"Maybe not, but that's never stopped me before. Both of you are acting like idiots. Jay, you need to calm down."

He turned his head and stared at her like she was speaking another language, thinking that out of everyone, at least she would have his back. She glared at him, then turned to Dave.

"And you need to think about what Jay said, and what you did, and then ask yourself why the hell you did it."

"You saw him, how he acted! I came down here to apologize—"

"Stop. Just knock it off. Nobody wants to hear you apologize, Dave, not unless you know what the fuck you're apologizing for."

Dave's mouth opened, for another rebuttal, Jay was sure, but he snapped it shut when the medic alarm rang. He shook his head and said nothing, just turned to leave and hurried up the steps.

Jay sank down on the weight bench and dropped his head into his hands, his breathing still heavy and strained. He felt Mike's eyes on him, waited for her to say something, but silence filled the room. She finally sat down next to him, her sigh heavy and depressed.

"I wish I knew what to say, Jay."

"Nothing. There's nothing to say."

She sighed again and leaned her head against his shoulder then straightened with a muttered curse. "Damn, you stink."

Jay laughed, the sound forced and hollow, and raised his head to give her a grateful smile. The smile fell flat, and he saw worry flash in her eyes.

"I'm here for you, buddy, you know that. What can I do for you? What do you need?"

Jay shook his head and looked away, his gaze settling on the concrete floor beneath his boots.

"Time. Just...time."

**

Duffy's was crowded again, the live music bringing in the people and the alcohol helping keep them there. Angie and Rick had been busy all night, aided by Grant, the bar's owner. The extra pair of hands helped, and Angie didn't want to think about how crazy it would be with just two of them.

The downside was that she had more time to think during the rare lull in the rush. She didn't want time to think.

So she made sure to keep busy, including running back to the large walk-in to grab extra cases of beer. She lowered the last one to the counter then leaned over and pushed open the top of the cooler, rotating the bottles before filling it. Then she broke down the empty case and looked up, making sure there were no waiting guests, before letting her eyes search the crowd.

Again.

She tried to ignore the pang of disappointment that filled her and called herself all kinds of stupid. Because even if Jay was here, it's not like she could talk to him.

Not like she would even know what to say to him.

She stacked the empty boxes together then walked to the rear of the bar and placed them on the pile of the other broken down cardboard. Either her or Rick would take them out to the recycle bin later, just before they closed.

Angie made her way back to the front of the bar and took a minute to stretch her back, feeling her tight muscles loosen, if only briefly. She used the chance to search the crowd again, her eyes focusing on the corner table. Everyone else Jay worked with was there, even her brother.

Everyone but Jay.

She sighed and reached for her glass of soda, taking a sip.

"If you're looking for Jay, don't bother. He won't be here tonight."

The voice startled her and Angie nearly dropped the glass in her hand. Her fingers tightened around it and she carefully placed it on the back counter then turned, only partially surprised to see Mike leaning against the bar.

Guilt filled her and she wondered how much the woman knew, wondered how much Jay had told her. "I, uh, wasn't looking for Jay."

The delicate brows arched above clear blue eyes in question. Or maybe it was doubt, Angie didn't know. But the woman didn't say anything, just ordered another round for the group.

She didn't bother with small talk, not knowing what she would say anyway, and busied herself with pulling beer from the cooler. The woman watched her, then turned back to look at her friends at the corner table.

"Your brother looks like he's having fun."

Angie looked up in surprise at the words, then glanced over at the table and felt a small smile form on her face. "Yeah, he is. That's good to see, at least."

"Your brother's an ass."

Angie spun to face the woman, certain her surprise was evident. Surprise, and a flash of irritation at the accusation. "He's not—"

"Really? Maybe, maybe not. I just find it funny that you're over here, looking completely miserable, while he's over there having fun. Makes me wonder what happened, you know?"

Mike watched her for a long minute, her clear eyes seeing too much before she grabbed the tray and stepped away. Angie watched her progress through the crowd, feeling a tinge of jealousy when Nick dropped a kiss on her cheek before moving toward the makeshift stage.

She wondered what it would be like, to be in a relationship like theirs, because it was obvious to even the most casual observer how much they loved each other. Jay had told her a little bit about their story and she knew that it hadn't been easy between them, but they had stuck it out and worked through it.

Guilt washed over her again but she pushed it away. She had done the right thing, she knew she had. There was no more tension between Dave and Jay, no more tension for either of them at work.

And no more tension between her and Dave at home. In fact, it was like the last several months had never happened. No, he hadn't stopped giving her grief about working at the bar but it was no longer a continual battle, and for that she was grateful.

But Mike was right. She was miserable.

And had been since telling Jay goodbye two weeks ago.

How much longer before she didn't feel a stab of pain every time she thought about him? How much longer before she would stop thinking about him?

She reached for her soda and drained it, then refilled it and sat it back on the counter. The band was warming up and the crowd was getting thicker around the bar, the patrons wanting to get one last order in before enjoying the music.

Angie went on auto-pilot, opening bottles and mixing drinks as quickly as Rick and Grant, knocking the lines back with little effort. And once again, Angie's eyes searched the crowd, looking for a head of dark blonde hair and a set of gray eyes.

"Who are you looking for?"

Angie jumped at the voice at her elbow then turned to find Dave watching her. She shook her head, feeling like she had just been caught doing something wrong and not liking the feeling one bit.

"Nobody, just checking out the crowd. Did you need another drink already?"

Dave held up the bottle, showing her it was almost full. "No, I just came over to remind you about taking off for the camping trip. It's next week."

She swore under her breath, having completely forgotten about the trip. There was no way she was going, not now, not after everything that had happened. She opened her mouth to tell Dave that but was stopped from saying anything when Rick stopped beside her.

"Already taken care of, pal. Told you I'd make sure she was off."

Angie stared after him as he moved away, then turned a furious look to her brother. "You asked Rick to give me the time off?"

"Of course. I knew you'd forget, and that's what big brothers do."

"No, Dave, it's not. Dammit, why do you have to keep trying to run my life? Did you think that maybe I didn't want to go?"

He watched her, his eyes questioning, and she realized that, in his mind, he did nothing wrong. He took a swallow of his beer then shook his head, giving her a smile. "Of course you want to go. You've gone every year. It'll be fun, like always."

"Dave, I don't want to go. And I'm not—"

But the band started playing, drowning out her words, and Dave walked away without even acknowledging anything she had said.

She stared after him, the realization slowly dawning on her that she needed to take control of her life, because if she didn't, Dave would keep on doing it.

But she had no idea how to do it, not when everything she had tried so far had failed.

Well, no more. And she'd prove it by not going on that trip.

She couldn't go, for many reasons.

The biggest reason of all was Jay.

And Dave would not force her into changing her mind.

Chapter Twenty

Vibrant greens whirled by, occasionally breaking to show a glimpse of valley, a flash of sunlight on deep green and brown below before coming together and soaring up, disappearing into shadow.

Angie leaned her head against the seat and stared out the window, watching the scenery pass by as they sped along I64 in West Virginia. She supposed the explosion of nature passing them by should fill her with a sense of peace and calm.

She was anything but.

Dave had won. Again. And now they were nearly to their destination, a partially wooded property tucked between Fayetteville and Park Service property in the New River Gorge that one of his friends owned. The back of Dave's truck was loaded up: tents, sleeping bags and air mattresses, firewood, cooler. Two duffel bags, one packed hastily and without much thought.

You'd think they were heading to a month-long excursion in the middle of nowhere, instead of a three-night getaway on the edge of small-town civilization.

Three nights. Angie repeated the words in her mind, telling herself she could handle this for three nights. They'd be back home by Thursday, since Dave and everyone else on his shift had to work on Friday. Surely she could handle three nights.

"How long before you get over your snit? It's been almost six hours, hasn't that been long enough?"

Angie turned her head and stared at Dave, her look letting him know in no uncertain terms that no, it wasn't long enough. But just in case he didn't get that, she said, "I'll be over my snit on Thursday when we get back home."

"I don't get it. What is wrong with you?"

"What's wrong with me?" She leaned over and turned the radio down, then turned in her seat. "What's wrong is that I didn't want to come on this trip. I told you that. But you wouldn't listen, as usual."

"You're just being hard-headed. You've come the last couple of years and had fun. I don't understand why you're being difficult."

"Difficult? Dave! What part of 'I don't want to go' didn't you understand? Why is it you always have this need to decide what it is I want without even asking me? Why do you feel like you need to control my life?"

He turned his head and looked at her, then went back to focusing on the road in front of them. His phone buzzed in its holder and he grabbed it. A frown creased his face, his mouth tightening into a hard line as he powered the phone down and tossed it on the dash. Angie was about to ask him who was texting him and if anything was wrong but he started talking before she could, picking right up where they left off.

And of course, he only picked up on what he wanted to hear, not what she was saying. "Again, I don't understand why you didn't want to go. A lot of the guys are bringing friends or family. It'll be fun, just like always."

"Are you really that stupid?"

His head whipped around and he glanced at her, surprise and dismay clear on his face. "Maybe I am. Maybe you should explain because I really don't see what the issue is."

"Really Dave? You think being forced to spend four days in the middle of the woods with a guy I'm no longer seeing is a good idea?"

He tossed her another look, a frown deepening the lines on his face, and she secretly rejoiced. Finally, he understood! She just wished he had seen the light six hours ago before he forced her along.

"Is that what this is about? You're worried about Jay? Well don't be. He's fine and I'm sure he won't even notice you're there. I wouldn't be surprised if he brings someone with him, because he always has before."

Angie sat back like she had been slapped. His words cut through her, piercing and sharp, and she swallowed against the emotion that choked her. She hadn't even thought, hadn't even considered the possibility that Jay might bring a date. And oh God, what would she do then? There was no way she could stay, no way she could act like that wouldn't bother her.

And Dave, damn him, still didn't understand.

"You know, Mike was right. You really are an

ass."

"What the hell is that supposed to mean?"

"Don't you ever stop and think before you say anything, Dave?"

"Think about what?" He glanced over at her and she wondered if he could tell she was upset, that his words hurt more than even she thought they would. He lowered his brows, worry creasing his forehead, then turned his gaze back to the road. Silence filled the truck for so long that Angie shifted in the seat and leaned her head back, closing her eyes.

"You're not going to tell me that you're upset about Jay. I told you before he wasn't your type, that it wouldn't work out. And I was right."

She didn't even bother to open her eyes or look at him, just turned her head further to the side.

"Whatever, Dave. You know best."

He must have missed the sarcasm in her words, must have missed the choked emotion in her voice, because he leaned over and patted her leg like she was a little kid.

"I know. Don't worry, you'll have fun. You won't even notice Jay's there."

**

"Are you fucking kidding me?" The words left Jay's mouth before he even realized he was speaking them. Mike looked over at him, then turned to watch the truck bouncing along the rutted path to the clearing. She stiffened beside him, her surprise as clear as his own.

"Well, this could be a good thing."

"I don't think so." He turned back to the tent he had just set up and started yanking at the pegs, ripping them from the dirt. Mike grabbed his arm, stopping him.

"What are you doing?"

"I'm leaving."

"Jay, you can't be serious."

"Yeah? Watch me."

Mike tugged on his arm again, pulling him away from the tent. She glanced back at the truck as it rolled to a slow stop, then turned back to him. "You can't leave."

"Mikey, there is no way in hell I'm staying here if Angie's going to be here. With her brother. I can't do it."

She studied his face, her eyes searching, seeing too much, then released the hold on his arm. "Fine. I think you'd be a fool to leave but if that's what you want, then go."

Jay turned, ready to tear down his tent again, then stopped and blew out a heavy breath. He straightened then looked back at Mike with a curse. "Why don't you think I should leave?"

A deep chuckle came from behind him and he turned to see Nick step closer. He gave Mike a quick kiss then smiled at Jay, his grin teasing. "Jay, you of all people should know when Kayla has an ulterior motive."

Mike playfully nudged Nick in the side and shook her head, telling him to stop. Jay looked away, their casual interplay striking a need deep inside him, a need he didn't want to admit to but could no longer ignore. He wanted what they had: friendship, respect, admiration. And love, a deep, profound love.

The thought jarred him, sending alternating waves of hot and cold through him until they joined and formed a huge knot in his gut. He looked over at the truck and watched as Angie climbed down and shut the door, pausing to glance around the campsite.

Her eyes met his and he felt his gut clench and twist even more as their gazes held. Longing scorched him, the strength and need of the emotion mentally flooring him.

Angie broke the contact and looked away, her gaze suddenly focused on the uneven ground at her feet. Jay inhaled deeply, a steadying breath to counter the imbalance he felt from just that one look.

"That's why, right there."

He looked over to see Mike grinning up at him. "What are you talking about?"

"That whole look. Jay, you've got it bad for Angie. Just like she has it bad for you."

"Newsflash, Mike. We're not seeing each other anymore, remember? Because *she* broke it off."

"Yeah, because of Dave, not because she wanted to."

"And your point is?"

"My point is: I've never seen you give up so easily. Since when do you not go after something you want?"

"Since it was made perfectly clear that it wasn't going to work. I know better than to beat a dead horse—unlike someone else I know." Jay kicked at the peg he had partially pulled up, then stomped it back into the ground with the heel of his boot, calling himself every kind of fool. He should be packing his tent up, calling it quits and heading home.

But he didn't.

Mike kept grinning at him as she lowered herself into the camp chair then leaned back and watched him. "I'm not beating a dead horse. I just don't want you to quit when I know how much you want it. How much both of you want it."

"Kayla, don't push." Nick leaned over and gave her another kiss. "I'm going to get something to drink. You two kids behave while I'm gone."

Jay swore to himself then grabbed his camp chair from the ground next to his tent, pulled it from the bag and set it up. Mike was watching him, a grin on her face as he slammed the chair into place before falling back into it.

Mike didn't say anything, just watched him with that stupid know-it-all grin he hated so much. She looked up as Nick approached with three bottles in his hands and took the soda he held out for her. Jay accepted the lone beer and twisted off the cap, taking a long swallow and trying not to look over at Angie.

But his eyes searched her out anyway and he watched as she started pulling gear from the back of Dave's truck. From the look on her face, she didn't want to be there.

He couldn't say he blamed her.

"Don't give up, Jay. You two are good together." Mike's voice was suddenly quiet, serious, and he looked over at her, surprised. He hadn't talked to her much about Angie, about how he thought he was feeling and what he was thinking. With Mike, he didn't need to. She knew him better than anyone else.

He looked away and took another swallow of beer, then shook his head. "It's not that easy, Mikey. Not with Dave acting so self-righteous."

"Yeah. And what the hell is up with that anyway? He's not usually such an ass."

"Gee, I don't know. Maybe it has something to

do with Angie being his little sister." Jay couldn't keep the sarcasm from his voice, surprised that he was even defending the man, not after everything that had happened. But Mike shook her head, her gaze thoughtful as she looked over where Dave was pitching his tent.

"No, there's something more going on. I told you that. He hasn't been himself for the last couple of months, even before you started seeing Angie. I just think that made whatever's going on worse."

"Gee, thanks Mikey. That makes me feel so much better."

She started then looked over at him, a small grin on her face. "Sorry, didn't mean it that way."

Jay really didn't feel like keeping this particular conversation going, so he let it slide and said nothing. He turned back and looked around the campsite, thinking that it was starting to look some kind of refugee camp.

Tents were scattered in a loose semi-circle around a large fire pit, camp chairs and coolers and gear tossed in between. A large brick grill stood on the other side of the fire pit, with a large screened tent set up next to it that housed two picnic tables. About fifty feet behind the tents, backing against the woods for privacy, was a portable shower and two latrines. Not exactly the height of luxury, but they were clean and functional, which is all they needed for the time they'd be out here.

The shift had been coming here for several years, ever since Pete had gotten the property from his grandparents. Jay had no idea if he ever planned on building on it or not, but the secluded acreage was perfect for these summer camping trips, and everyone had always had a blast.

Jay had a feeling this year would be the exception for him.

He took another swig of beer then let his eyes drift back to where Angie was standing. Her hair was pulled back in a loose ponytail and a few strands had come free, waving around her cheek in the slight breeze. She stood off to the side, looking uncomfortable and out of place as she watched Dave set up their tent.

Jay did a double-take then choked on the beer he had been swallowing. The tent Dave was setting up was a two-person tent—which meant it was really only big enough for one person. There was no way in hell both of them could sleep in that thing.

His eyes searched the gear piled around Dave's tent, coming to rest on another bag as memory of the last few years' trips came back to him. This wasn't the first time Angie had joined Dave on the trip. And each year before, they had each had their own tent.

He wasn't sure why he was just now remembering that, or why the realization made him happy. And he sure as hell wasn't going to waste time thinking about it.

"Hey Jimmy, can you give Angie a hand with her tent?" Dave looked up and called across the clearing, where Jimmy and Pete were wrestling with what was supposed to be tonight's dinner.

Pete looked over at him then shook his head, his gloved hands smeared with sauce and seasoning. "The chefs are busy." His eyes darted around the campsite, stopping to rest on Jay. "Have Jay or Mike do it. And her tent can't go next to yours."

"Why the hell not?"

"Because we need to leave that area clear for the vehicles. You know that."

Jay watched the exchange with a sinking feeling and shifted in his chair. He looked around the camp and suddenly saw what had been obvious to Pete.

A semi-circle of nine tents. The fire pit. The grill and eating tent. A clearing for the cars and trucks.

And the next empty spot was right next to Jay's, since he had been the last one to show up.

Right before Dave.

"Shit." He lifted the bottle to his mouth and drained the beer, afraid to look around, afraid to look over at Angie, afraid that Dave was ready to lose his shit.

He heard Mike laugh next to him but he wouldn't even look at her.

"I love it. This is great." She laughed again and pushed herself out of the chair, then walked the fifty feet separating them from Dave's tent. Jay watched as she said something to Angie, then grabbed her gear and led the way toward them.

Jay shifted in his seat again and swore. "Sometimes I really hate your girlfriend."

Nick laughed and offered him a sympathetic smile. "You know how she gets once she has an idea stuck in her head. Stubborn doesn't even come close."

"Tell me about it," he muttered.

Mike finally reached them, a glint of mischief in her eyes as she glanced at Jay. Angie stopped behind her, looking as uncomfortable as he felt. He glanced back at Mike, wondering how to tell her this wasn't a good idea.

"This is probably a bad idea."

Jay snapped his mouth shut as a flare of irritation

went through him. His gaze shot to Angie and he almost asked her why she thought it was a bad idea.

Almost. But he couldn't ignore the misery and discomfort on her face, and he wouldn't add to it. He sat the empty bottle in the chair's cup holder and stood up, holding his hand out to Mike.

"Mikey, why don't you and Nick grab two more beers while I help Angie?"

Mike all but threw the tent bag at him and quickly walked away, not bothering to hide her smile as she hurried past him. Angie didn't notice, though, because her gaze was locked on his.

"I know how to set up a tent, you don't need to help."

"No worries." He watched her for another second, trying not to notice how her arms were crossed so tightly in front of her, a sure sign of discomfort. He looked away and upended the bag then sorted through everything. "Do you have a ground cover?"

"Oh. Um, yeah, it's in here." She bent over and rummaged through another bag, then pulled out the small tarp. He reached out for it, his hands brushing against hers and sending a shot of awareness up his arm. Their eyes met and they both just stood there, watching each other. Angie was the first to look away, a faint blush coloring her cheeks.

Jay cleared his throat then busied himself with laying out the ground cover and spreading out the tent. Angie bent over, helping him straighten it, then handed him the pegs.

"Let's get the poles in first and set it, then we can put the pegs down." Angie didn't say anything, just nodded and started assembling the poles, sliding them together one at a time. Jay sat back on his heels and watched her, his gaze travelling along her body. Even dressed as she was, in loose shorts, an unbuttoned shirt hanging open over a tank shirt, and hiking boots, she heated his blood.

He cleared his throat again and looked away. "You look good, Angie."

Silence greeted his comment and he mentally kicked himself for saying anything, then wondered if the next four days were going to be just like this. He didn't think he could handle it if they were.

"Thanks. You too. Look good, I mean."

Jay looked over at her and saw that she was staring down at the pole in her hands, another flush high on her cheeks. She took a deep breath then finally met his gaze, her discomfort clear.

"I don't have to put my tent here, I can find someplace else. I, uh, I don't want to..." Her voice drifted off and she looked away, the flush growing deeper.

"You don't want to what?"

"You know. Impose. Get in your way."

He held out his hand for the pole, almost surprised that she gave it to him. He ran it through the nylon sleeve and hooked it into the grommet, then looked back at her. "Why would you think you'd be in my way or imposing?"

"Oh. Well." She looked around, her gaze darting around the campsite before settling on his tent. She narrowed her eyes and looked over her shoulder, in the direction of her brother, then back down at him. Her eyes didn't meet his, though, just settled on a spot somewhere over his shoulder. "Dave said you'd probably have someone with you."

"Dave said. Of course he did." Jay clenched his jaw and shoved the other pole through the sleeve, using care not to tear the nylon even though he wanted to throw the damn thing like a javelin.

Preferably straight through her brother.

He stood up and brushed at his leg then looked back at Angie. "I didn't bring anyone with me, Angie. There's nobody I'd want to bring, and I haven't seen anyone else since—I'm not seeing anyone. I have no interest in seeing anyone. So don't worry, you're not going to be imposing or in my way."

And damn his big mouth. For not planning on saying anything, he sure as hell just said a lot. He shook his head and grabbed the last pole, then leaned over and slid it in place.

"I'm not either." The words were spoken quickly, almost as if the speaker was afraid to say them and had to spit them out before thinking better of it. Jay looked over and met Angie's eyes, noticed the rigid set to her shoulders and arms, and realized that she was already regretting speaking.

"Great. Glad we're both miserable." He shook his head and motioned for her to grab one side of the tent, then lifted and set it in place. He didn't bother looking at her again, didn't want to see what effect his sarcastic words had on her, if they had any effect at all. He grabbed the pegs and walked around the tent, setting each in place and sinking them with the heel of his boot.

"Do you have an air mattress?"

"Yeah, it's right here." She handed him another bag and he took it, still without looking at her. He pulled the mattress out then turned toward the tent, planning on rolling it out once inside then inflating it.

A strong hand clamped down on his shoulder, stopping it.

"Don't worry, Jay, I've got it."

He glanced down at the hand gripping his shoulder, then up at Dave. His expression was bland, but warning was clear in his eyes. Jay shrugged his hand off and tossed the air mattress at him.

"Whatever you say, Dave."

He turned around and walked away, his jaw clenched and anger ringing in his ears. But he still heard Angie's deep sigh, heard her swear at her brother in a whisper. He turned to watch her and almost smiled when she ripped the air mattress from Dave's hand and disappeared inside the tent, telling him she would do it herself.

Almost smiled. But not quite. He kept walking, straight pass Mike and Nick, heading for his truck. He heard footsteps behind him, racing to catch up, but he didn't stop until he opened the door of his truck.

"Jay, where are you going?"

"Into town. I need a drink."

Mike's expression told him exactly what she thought—that he was a coward and running away. He wasn't going to argue with her, even though there was a bit more to it than that. He just needed to get away for a little bit, to put some distance between him and Angie—and Dave—before he did something really stupid. If she wanted to call it running away, he wasn't going to stop her.

He climbed into the truck then looked down at her. "You coming?"

She rolled her eyes then turned back to Nick, an entire conversation passing between them with that one quick look. Nick waved at them and she hurried around to the other side, climbing into the passenger seat and settling in. She snapped the seat belt around her as Jay started the truck and backed up.

"The only reason I'm not arguing with you is because this means I'll get to drive the truck back. You know that, right?"

Jay said nothing, because there was nothing to say. She was right, because he meant it when he said he was going into town to get a drink.

Probably several.

Maybe then he'd be able to sleep tonight without thinking about Angie curled in the tent next to his.

Chapter Twenty-One

Darkness had descended over the campsite, night dragging its shadows across the clearing. Branches scratched against each other around them and the sounds of furtive scampering in the underbrush whispered in the woods behind them. Animal songs murmured in the night, occasionally cut short with a tiny shriek.

Sitting there around the campfire, her arms wrapped around her to ward off the slight chill of the mountain air, Angie was certain of two things. First, if not for the blazing fire and the laughing group surrounding it, an essentially isolated clearing of land in the middle of nowhere West Virginia would be frightening.

And second, no matter how many people were gathered around, quietly talking or laughing, she had never before felt like such an outsider.

She glanced down at the empty bottle in her hand and thought about getting up to get another wine cooler. Then she wondered if that would be

"And why did you have to pack so fast?"

"Because I hadn't planned on coming, didn't want to."

Jay still watched her and she was afraid his eyes saw so much more than she wanted him to see. She looked away, studying the bottle in her hand, knowing she should just put it back and go to sleep.

But Jay reached for the bottle with his free hand and held it in the crook of his elbow to twist the cap off. He handed it back to her, and she briefly wondered if he had been reading her mind and thought that opening the bottle would keep her from running to her tent.

No. More likely, he was just trying to be polite.

"So if you didn't want to come, why did you?"

The question surprised her, because she didn't think he'd really care. Not about the answer, not even about making small talk. There was no reason for him to even be here talking to her, not after everything she'd done.

But she couldn't bring herself to walk away, not again. No matter how hard it was to stand this close to him and not touch him.

"I didn't have much choice. Dave pretty much told me I was coming."

"And we all know you do whatever big brother says to do." Anger flashed in his eyes and laced his words, sharp and biting. Angie flinched, knowing he had a right to his anger, had a right to feel that way.

But it surprised her anyway. Surprised her that he would feel so strongly, surprised her that part of her actually understood it.

And agreed with him.

She opened her mouth to say something then

immediately closed it. There wasn't anything she could say, nothing that would make any difference, or make anything better.

"Shit. Angie, I'm sorry. I didn't mean—"

"No, it's okay. Really."

They stood there, neither one talking, not even really looking at each other. Angie wondered how long it would be before either of them moved, knowing that it was just a matter of time. And how sad was it that she didn't want to leave? That this new tension between them didn't matter, as long as she could just be near him, if only for a few minutes.

Jay shifted and muttered under his breath, then pushed his bottle toward her. "Here, hold this."

She grabbed it right before it could fall, then watched as Jay reached down and grabbed the hem of his sweatshirt. He yanked it over his head and her eyes drifted down, resting on the bare skin of his abdomen as his t-shirt pulled up. But the cotton material fell back in place when he lowered his arms, turning the sweatshirt right side out. Jay took the beer from her hand, then thrust his sweatshirt in its place.

"Put this on before you freeze to death."

Angie looked down at the shirt in her hand then up at Jay. His jaw was clenched as he stared past her, his gaze focused on the group behind them. Firelight reflected in his eyes, turning them from the color of flint to a warm blue-gray.

She sat her bottle on the cooler then pulled the sweatshirt over her head. Heat from Jay's body surrounded her and she breathed in deep, inhaling the exotic mix of wood smoke and spice and pure male that was all Jay.

"I didn't think it'd be that big on you."

Angie looked up and felt her breath lodge in her throat at the intensity in Jay's eyes. Then he blinked, and whatever emotion she thought she saw was gone. He sat his beer down next to hers then grabbed the sleeves of the shirt. They hung well past her fingers, the shirt three sizes too big, and she wanted to tell him she didn't mind but it was too late, because he was already rolling the sleeves up to her wrists. His fingers brushed against hers and she thought that maybe he held them for just a second, squeezing them.

But then his hands were gone and he was reaching down for both bottles. He handed her the wine cooler then walked away without saying a word, leaving her staring after him, wondering what had just happened.

Wondering if she had imagined the flare of heat in his eyes when he touched her. Wondering if she had really seen the need in his expression, or the flare of pain when he looked at her.

Wondering if she had really seen those things, or if it was nothing more than a reflection of what she was feeling herself.

Chapter Twenty-Two

The rush of fast-flowing water echoed in the gorge around them. The sun hadn't quite made it over the mountains yet and a swirling fog hovered over the river in front of them, cloaking everything in a mystery known only to Mother Nature. Jay inhaled deeply, enjoying the mingled scents of damp earth and green foliage. Somebody smacked him from behind and he stumbled forward, catching himself at the last minute before he sprawled face-first over a fallen log.

"It's too freaking early to be communing with nature, so knock it off." Jimmy grumbled, pushing past Jay to sit on the log he had almost tripped over.

"What's the matter, Jimmy? Head hurt?"

Jay laughed at the expression Jimmy gave him. He couldn't help that he was in a good mood.

Despite the early hour.

Despite the barely-there throbbing at the base of his skull.

He looked behind him and saw the rest of their

small group moving along the trail, each carrying a paddle and either wearing or carrying a helmet and floatation vest. There were eight total that had decided to go on the rafting trip.

And Dave wasn't among them.

Jay smiled again as the group gathered around, his gaze resting on Angie. Her face was just a little pale, her eyes wide as they looked around—and stopped on him. She offered him a hesitant smile then looked over at the two river guides who were just finishing the raft preparations.

Jay moved through the small crowd, not stopping until he reached Mike. She looked up at him and rolled her eyes. "I know, I know. You don't have to say anything. It'll be us four in one raft, I got it. Now shut up so I can listen to the instructions."

Jay laughed and turned back around but he wasn't paying attention as much as some of the others were. He'd done this before, knew what the guides were saying. Pete grimaced at some of the instructions then turned back to Jay.

"Shit, we're all going to die. Don't stand. Feet up. Curl into a ball. Stay away from undercut rocks. Whose freaking idea was this, anyway?"

Jay laughed again, his eyes settling on Angie. She wore the same expression as Jimmy, only he was pretty sure hers wasn't the result of a hangover. He made his way over to her, smiling when she looked up at him.

"Ferris wheel?"

She blinked at the question, then realization sparked in her eyes. She glanced over at the rafts, to the river beyond, then back at Jay. Her mouth tilted, ever so slightly, at one corner as she shook her head.

"No. At least, I don't think so. I've never done this before."

"You'll be fine, don't worry. It's fun."

"I take it that means you've gone white water rafting before?"

"A few times."

Angie nodded but didn't say anything, and Jay couldn't help but notice that something resembling relief crossed her face. He bit back his smile, listening to the river guides as they finished their talk. Then it was time to put the rafts in the water and move out.

Jay was careful not to be too obvious, but it was easier than he thought it would be to make sure Angie was in the same raft with him and Mikey and Nick. Actually, Angie just drifted over and joined them, not even bothering to look at the rest of the guys.

Jay told himself not to read too much into it.

"Hey, something is not right with this. Why are both women in the same raft? Moore, get over here, I want to switch," Pete called. Jay laughed and shook his head as he climbed onto the raft.

"No way Miller. If I'm going to die, I want to be surrounded by pretty scenery."

"You're going to get a paddle upside the head if you don't shut-up." Mike settled on the side next to him and across from Angie, then turned and frowned when she noticed the seating arrangement. "Angie, let's switch."

Jay smothered his smile as the two women changed places, the raft rocking under the motion. Their guide, Mark, took them through the basic paddling instructions, making sure everyone worked together, then they started downstream, heading into the early morning mist.

Jay looked back and noticed that Pete, Jimmy, Adam and Dale were still arguing over who was going to sit where, then he laughed when their guide started issuing orders and telling them to just get in. He knew their own raft wouldn't go too far ahead and sure enough, they headed closer to the bank just a few minutes into the trip to wait.

Jay rested the paddle across his lap and looked around, taking in the abundance around them. The ground lifted on either side of the river, pine and oak growing thick and green. He squinted and looked downriver, seeing the outline of the steeper cliffs as the mountains grew taller and more rugged. He looked down and noticed Angie watching him with a smile.

"It is gorgeous, isn't it?"

He nodded, then looked over at Mike and Nick. "What do you think so far?"

"I'll let you know once we get started, okay?" Mike still didn't look thrilled at the adventure, so Nick reached out and gave her a reassuring squeeze.

Shouts greeted them from behind and Jay turned to see the other raft finally moving their way. Mark leaned forward, giving them instructions as they pushed back into the current. Their first rapid was coming up, an easy Class I. Jay glanced over at Angie, saw the slight tightening of her mouth as she mentally prepared herself.

Then they were there. Paddle, paddle, paddle. Stop.

And done. Jay laughed at the nearly identical expressions on both Mike's and Angie's faces as they looked behind them, surprised to hear they had just shot their first rapid.

"That was it?" Angie asked, almost looking disappointment.

"We've got some bigger ones coming up, don't worry. Just keep doing what you did, and it'll be a piece of cake," Mark assured them.

Angie looked over her shoulder at Jay, her smile bright, excitement now clear on her face. He felt an answering smile on his own face and realized this was probably one of the best ideas he had come up with yet.

**

The morning passed quickly. The sun rose higher, burning off the last of the mist, and beat down on them, hot and bright. Jay adjusted the strap on his sunglasses then sat them back on his face, making sure they were secure. They weren't his best pair, but that didn't mean he wanted to lose them.

"Alright guys, we've got a Class IV coming up. We can take the easy way and shoot straight through, or we can get a little crazy. What do you guys want to do?"

Angie and Mike exchanged glances, then looked back at Mark.

"Get a little crazy," they said in unison. Jay looked over at Nick, one eyebrow raised in amusement.

"I think they're getting a little cocky."

"Hey, this was your idea. I'm putting the blame squarely on your shoulders."

Jay laughed and shifted, repositioning his feet so he was more balanced on the raft. Mark gave them instructions on which way they would paddle, and what to expect each minute, along with what to do if they fell out.

Get back to the raft, or aim for the middle—away from the undercut rocks near the bank.

Everyone dipped their paddles in, waiting, then Mark shouted his instructions and everyone dug in, pulling harder as the raft shot forward. Waves of water pummeled them, pushing and pulling at the raft as it tumbled left then right, sailing over a rock then coming back down.

"Right side forward, left side back." Mark's voice carried over the roar of thousands of gallons of water forcing its way between the rocks. Jay's paddle met air as the raft went airborne then landed nose first. The right side, their side, scraped against a boulder and tilted up, up. Jay dug his foot in and leaned back as the nose of the raft dipped down once more. A wall of water crashed over them, leaving everyone wet and sputtering before disappearing behind them.

Jay heard a surprised scream and turned forward just as Angie lost her balance. She wheeled her arms, her grip still tight on the paddle as she started falling backward. Jay lunged for her, his fingers just catching a strap of her jacket before she tumbled backward and disappeared into the water.

"Holy shit." Jay wasn't sure who yelled, didn't care as his heart dropped into his stomach, fear holding him in an icy death grip. His eyes scanned the water, searching for signs of Angie. Her paddle broke the surface, straight up like some misplaced street sign, but he didn't see her.

And then he realized she was still holding onto the paddle as the river swept her away.

"Paddle, paddle, paddle!" Mark shouted the instructions, leaning hard on his paddle to steer them through the rapids. Jay didn't know where he found the strength, only knew that they had to paddle, that if they didn't, they wouldn't reach Angie in time.

He muttered a prayer over and over, watching as that lone paddle moved downstream, shifting away from the middle and closer to the right bank, closer to the unforgiving, undercut rocks.

But Angie still hadn't surfaced and Jay's fear grew. She was alright, she had to be alright because she was still holding that damn paddle straight up. She had to be alright.

His arms burned as he dug deeper into the water, pulling with everything he had to reach Angie. And they would reach her, because the alternative was unbearable.

"Look, there!"

Jay looked in the direction Mike was indicating with a nod of her head and felt a sliver of short-lived relief when he saw Angie's head break the surface. Her eyes widened in shock before she turned onto her back, her feet stretched out in front of her. Her body bounced over another rock and she went under again, the water claiming her one more time.

"Faster! There's another Class IV coming up. Paddle, paddle."

Fear like he had never known before gripped Jay and he struggled to push it away, knowing only that he had to paddle—hard, fast—to reach Angie before her body was battered into the rocks.

She broke the surface once more, her arms flailing by her side, the paddle still in her hand. He watched her face harden in determination as she turned in the raging water then flipped over, now on her stomach, her feet kicking against the water as she aimed for the raft.

Then they were beside her and he was reaching down, paddle forgotten when his hands closed in a death grip on her vest as he pulled her in. She shot over the side and landed in a sprawled heap on top of him in the middle of the raft. Mike quickly shifted, taking Jay's spot on the raft as Mark called out instructions.

Paddle. Paddle. Paddle.

Stop.

And just like that, the water calmed, becoming nothing more than a flat surface that reflected the mountains looming on either side of them.

Jay closed his eyes and said a quick prayer, then scrambled to a sitting position. Angie was still sprawled on top of him, her chest moving up and down with heavy breaths.

"Angie, shit. Talk to me. Are you okay?"

She opened her eyes and looked at him for a long second, then a wide smile broke her face and shone brightly in her eyes.

"I didn't lose my paddle!"

Chapter Twenty-Three

Lunch was anything but subdued. In fact, the excitement almost resembled a party.

And Angie felt like the guest of honor.

Her swim through the rapid had been told and retold from everyone's perspective. From listening to them, it sounded like she had faced certain death and come out unscathed.

But she saw it from a different perspective, and didn't think it was quite that bad. Actually, all she could remember was water. Lots of water. Rushing over her, battering her, shooting her over and around rocks. Quiet words of reassurance, repeating themselves over and over in her mind. And the memory of Jay's face, his gray eyes intense as they watched over her.

Don't panic. Stay calm.

Keep your feet up.

Swim to the raft.

Don't panic. Stay calm.

The words in her head had been in Jay's voice.

Calming. Reassuring.

And then the rushing wall of water was gone and he was there, leaning over the side and pulling her into the raft, his strong arms tight around her, protecting, comforting, as they went through another rapid.

Yes, her perspective was just a little different than everyone else's. And while she was in no hurry to repeat the experience, she had to admit that it had been pretty exciting.

"Are you sure you're okay?"

Jay placed his plate of food on the table, then straddled the bench next to her.

"Yes, I'm fine. For the hundredth time."

"How's your thumb?"

Angie looked down at the only injury she had suffered, a small avulsion to the fleshy part between her right thumb and forefinger. She held her hand up and waved it front of him.

"All better, see? Jimmy bandaged it for me."

"Yeah, Jay. Give it a break. I do know what I'm doing, you know."

Jay shot him a dirty look then turned back to her. He opened his mouth but Angie stopped him with a smile.

"I'm fine. Now eat before your burger gets cold."

She turned back to her own plate and took another bite of the potato salad. Lunch was included in the trip and nobody hesitated to attack the food. Including her.

It was funny how hungry body surfing a Class IV rapid could make someone.

Angie shook her head and almost laughed. If she wasn't careful, she'd start believing the exaggerated retellings of the entire event.

"I got to tell you, Angie, that really was impressive. The way you held your paddle up the entire time? I wish I had a camera." Adam laughed as he walked by her. It was the most he had ever said to her, ever, and she couldn't help smiling at the feeling of fitting in, of belonging, that settled over her.

She wasn't just Dave's sister anymore. No, now she was actually one of them. It was weird and funny and left her with a warm tingly feeling all at the same time and she didn't know why.

Everyone was pretty much finished eating now and they were either hanging around talking and joking, or playing with the corn hole game that was set up on the other side of the picnic area. And while Angie thought it was nice that she seemed to be one of them now, she couldn't help but be grateful that there was nobody else around them just this minute.

It was just her and Jay.

Jay pushed his empty plate away then shifted closer to her, so close that his knees pushed against her thigh. His hand reached out and gently caressed her leg, heat instantly warming her as his eyes held hers. They were serious, deep and intense, and she shifted under the weight of his gaze.

"You scared the living hell out of me." His voice was pitched low, so low that she almost couldn't hear him. She hesitated, not sure what to do or say.

Then she just stopped thinking and placed her hand over his and threaded their fingers together.

"I'm sorry." She whispered the words, her gaze steady as she watched him, trying to let him know that she wasn't talking about her ride down the river. He watched her for long seconds, then his mouth tilted up in a grin and he squeezed her hand.

And just like that, the stress and tension that had been weighing on her for the last several weeks vanished. She had been foolish, so foolish, to call things off with Jay, not when he made her feel the way he did. And for what? Because her brother didn't approve? It wasn't the first time Dave hadn't approved of something she did. She had never let that stop her before, so why now? Had she used her brother's disapproval as an excuse because she was afraid of what she was feeling? Stupid. So stupid.

She leaned forward, her heart tripping in her chest, wanting to feel Jay's lips against hers. She closed her eyes, anticipation thick between them.

"You know, you two really do make a cute couple."

Angie jumped, startled, and looked around only to notice that pretty much everyone was suddenly watching them. Her face heated and she looked down, embarrassed.

"Pete, you're a fucking moron."

"What? What did I say?"

Angie heard a mix of voices and answers in reply but didn't pay any attention to them because all her focus was suddenly on Jay. He gripped her chin in his hand and tipped her head up, forcing her to look at him. And she was drawn in, losing herself in those mesmerizing eyes as he leaned forward and pressed his lips against hers.

Her heart skipped wildly and she felt a small moan in the back of her throat. She leaned toward him, trying to get closer, and placed her hand against his bare chest. Heat from his body singed her, his lips stirring the embers deep inside her to life.

"Damn. Now I know why Jay wanted her in the raft with him."

She felt Jay smile against her mouth just before he broke the kiss. He rested his forehead against hers, his shoulders shaking in soundless mirth. Angie squeezed his hand then straightened on the wooden bench, her face heating as she stared at the table, not quite able to look around.

Something flew across the field of her peripheral vision and she looked up in time to see the remains of a hamburger bun, coated with ketchup and mustard, hit Pete square in the chest. It stuck there for a split second then dropped to the ground, leaving a mixture of sauce glued to the center of his chest.

He groaned and wiped at the mess on his shirt, then looked over to see Mike shaking her head at him.

"You really are a moron, Pete."

And Angie laughed, the sound coming from deep inside her, clear and joyful as the last of her worries evaporated in the clear mountain air around them.

**

The bus bounced along the rutted road, jarring and swaying under them. Jay shifted then readjusted his hold around Angie, settling her head more comfortably against his chest.

He had no idea how she was even sleeping.

Granted, it had been a long day, starting as soon as everyone got up before six that morning. And it had been a day filled with fresh air, exertion, exercise, excitement.

Near drowning.

Jay closed his eyes and said another quick prayer of thanks to whoever was listening. He never wanted to feel that kind of fear again. Ever. Once was more than enough, more than he could bear to handle.

He dropped a kiss on the top of Angie's head and held her more tightly against him.

It was funny how something like that quickly put your priorities in perspective. He didn't think Angie yet realized how serious her swim downriver had been, how dangerous. How close she really came to serious injury or worse. But he did, and he was still shaken by it. And he realized, at the instant he thought he might never see her smile again, might never be able to hold her in his arms again, that Angie was his top priority. Screw work, screw Dave. His top priority was Angie, period.

And in that same instant he realized, with sharp clarity, that he loved her. It was as simple as that.

As terrifying and complicated as that.

He almost told her, when they had been sitting at the picnic table at lunch, but he stopped himself. He didn't want to tell her something so important, so earth-shatteringly profound, in front of a bunch of the guys from work. He wanted to save it for a tender, intimate moment, when it was just the two of them.

His brows lowered in a frown as he quickly rethought that. Maybe not intimate. He didn't want her to think he was declaring something so special in the middle of some passionate moment just because he was in the middle of that moment.

But he didn't want to share it in front of the guys he worked with, either.

He dropped another kiss on the top of her head then opened his eyes and looked up, surprised to see Nick studying him. He felt like he had been caught in the middle of doing something he shouldn't have been and awkwardly cleared his throat. But Nick kept studying him, his gaze darting between Jay and Angie.

"You going to tell her?" Nick's voice was pitched low, barely audible over the whine of the engine as they bounced once more. Jay automatically tightened his hold around Angie, and he noticed Nick did the same with Mike.

How in the hell were they both sleeping?

The bus jarred one more time, then the surface changed to asphalt, smoothing out under them.

Nick turned back and looked at him once more, repeating his earlier question. "So, are you going to tell her?"

"Tell her what?"

Nick raised one eyebrow at him, then shook his head and chuckled. "I can see it clear as day on your face. I know, because that's the same expression I see every morning and every night when I look in the mirror."

Jay smiled, just the barest of grins, and nodded. "Yeah, I guess you do. Damn good thing too, or else I'd have to kick your ass."

They both grinned at each other, grown men acting like love sick fools, and Jay was suddenly glad that nobody was paying them any attention. Or, if they were, that they couldn't hear what they were talking about. He glanced around, just in case. Just as he thought, everyone else was either dozing, or zoning out as they stared out the window.

"You know there's going to be a shit storm when we get back, right?"

"Yeah, probably."

"Any idea how you're going to handle it?"

Jay sighed and shook his head, then stared out the window as the bus barreled down Route 19, on its way back to the rafting center. He had no idea what was going to happen when they got back to the campsite, only knew that something would.

Because he had no intention of pretending today hadn't happened. No intention of pretending that Angie wasn't with him, that she wasn't his.

"I haven't thought that far ahead, but I'm sure I'll think of something."

"No you won't, because I will." The sleepy voice was muffled against his chest, but still loud enough for him to hear. He stiffened in surprised then moved his arm when Angie straightened next to him and stretched. She gave him a sleepy smile then leaned forward and placed a quick kiss against his lips.

"He's my brother, Jay. I'll handle this."

"Angie—"

She cut him off with another kiss then pulled back and stared deep into his eyes, her gaze almost pleading. "I know, I didn't handle it right the first time, which is why I need to talk to him, not you."

"That's not what I was going to say."

"I know." She ran her finger along his lower lip, her eyes almost sad. "But I have to, okay? I *need* to, Jay."

His eyes searched hers for a long minute before he blew out his breath. He didn't want her to have to deal with it, with any of it, but the unspoken need was clear in her eyes and he knew he wouldn't stop her.

Not unless he had to, and then he'd have no problem getting between her and Dave.

But he didn't say any of that, just sighed again and nodded. "Fine. You can talk to him. I just wish to hell I didn't suddenly feel like freaking Romeo and Juliet."

Nick turned around his seat and faced both of them, his expression just the tiniest bit amused. "You know they both died, right?"

"Thanks. Thanks a lot, Mr. English Lit teacher. Really? You couldn't come up with something better than that?" Jay didn't know whether to laugh or throw something at him. Considering he didn't have anything handy to throw, he chose to laugh.

But only a little, the sound just a bit forced. Because Nick's comment worried him a little too much. No, he didn't think things would escalate to the point of death, but Mike's words from yesterday came back to him.

Something *was* going on with Dave, and he had changed over the last several months. Jay had no idea what could have happened and he didn't think it was just because he and Angie had started seeing each other. No, there was something else.

He just didn't know what the hell it was.

They didn't have much time for more conversation because the bus turned off the highway, then turned again onto another semi-paved road that was barely wide enough for the bus to comfortably navigate. Five jarring minutes later, the bus pulled into the top parking lot of the rafting outfit and everyone piled out.

They still had to return their gear, and they had already planned on using the shower facilities there instead of the more primitive one back at the campsite. Because who would turn down hot water? That only took another five minutes. Well, at least for the guys. Angie and Mike were still in the women's locker room, doing only who knew what.

The six of them milled around outside, waiting, and Nick brought up the idea of eating at a nearby pizza and beer place. But Pete and Jimmy backed out, along with Adam and Dale, saying they had to get back to start dinner for everyone else anyway.

And Mike and Angie still hadn't come out.

"What are they doing in there?" Jay wondered.

"Talking."

"You sure about that?"

"Yeah, pretty sure. Kayla never takes this long to get ready unless we're going somewhere super nice and she has to get all dressed up. Even then, I don't think she takes this long."

"I wonder what the hell they're talking about?"

"I'm going to pretend you didn't even ask that. What do you think they're talking about?"

Jay mumbled beneath his breath, realizing even as he asked the question that they were probably talking about him. And he wasn't sure why, but that thought was a bit disconcerting.

He looked back toward the locker room, but there was still no sign of them.

"So have you given any more thought to what I said earlier?"

Jay turned back to Nick, not quite understanding the question until he met the other man's eyes. He rolled his shoulders then shrugged, not sure how to answer. Yes, he was going to tell Angie, but he wanted the time to be right, wanted the place to be right.

He opened his mouth to tell Nick that, to try to explain, when the door to the women's locker room finally opened and Angie and Mike walked out. Angie smiled at him and Jay completely forgot what he was going to say. He heard Nick chuckle behind him, and turned to look at him.

"Either way, I wouldn't worry. Because that expression I see in the mirror each day, that expression I see on your face?" He nodded toward Angie then smiled. "It's the same look I've seen on her on her face."

Chapter Twenty-Four

The truck bounced along the rutted path, the headlights veering up and down with each bump, shining a ribbon of light into a patch of darkness before moving to the next. The taillights of Mike's CJ7 had already disappeared in front of them and Angie was pretty sure that Jay was deliberately slowing, letting them get further ahead.

They hit another bump then Jay slowed even more, finally stopping. He put the truck in park, flipped the headlight switch to the dimmers, then turned in his seat and faced her. Lights from the instrument panel illuminated his face, the shadows carving out deeper hollows beneath his cheekbones. The corner of his mouth tilted in a slight grin as his hand closed around hers.

She reached over and unhooked the seatbelt, then leaned across the center console to meet him halfway. His mouth crashed on hers, hard and hungry, as his hand drifted through her hair and cupped the back of her head.

She ran her hand up along his chest, feeling the warmth of his skin and the steady pounding beat of his heart under her palm. Her mouth opened and his tongue swept in, thrusting against hers with an urgency that ignited a need that had been simmering for the last several hours.

Jay shifted in his seat, moving to get closer at the same time she was. She heard a bang, then Jay pulled away with a small groan that spoke of impatience and frustration. His eyes sparked in the half-darkness that engulfed them, reflecting the same need and desire flowing through her veins, burning her.

"I need you, Angie. God, you have no idea how much I need you." His voice was a whisper in the heavy air around them, the words a match that ignited something deep inside her, something hot, heavy, needy.

Desperate.

She pressed her lips against his, the kiss frantic with shared need, then pulled back with a harsh breath. She shifted in the passenger seat then reached for the hem of her t-shirt and pulled it over her head, then did the same with her sports bra. Damp night air came through the open window and kissed her flushed skin, a heady sensation of hot and cold. Jay's eyes caressed her, his gaze burning and bold as they dropped to her chest.

She watched him watching her, and felt powerful, beautiful, wanted. She dropped her hands to the waistband of her gym shorts and pushed them down, shifting in the seat and tilting her hips until the material slid past her legs to her ankles. She kicked them off then turned back to Jay. His chest rose and fell with heavy breaths as he watched her, desire burning in his eyes. Burning her.

He moaned then turned in the seat, threw the truck in reverse, then looked behind him as he backed up. She knew where he was going, to the small section of the path that widened.

He maneuvered the truck off the trail, coming dangerously close to the trees, then turned off the lights and killed the engine. Angie leaned across the console, needing to touch him, feel him. Her hands fisted in his shirt, pulling at it, wanting nothing between them. He pushed her hands out of the way and tore the shirt over his head, his breathing as ragged as hers. Then he grabbed her and pulled, until she was sprawled partly across the console and his lap.

His mouth crashed against hers, demanding response, demanding surrender. He dragged his hand down her side, down until he reached between her legs, his fingers spreading her, stroking her. She opened her legs as fire raced through her, burning, searing.

She shifted, reached down and tugged at his sweatpants, reached in and grabbed him. Her fingers closed over his hard length and she stroked him, her grip hard, desperate.

Jay pulled his mouth from hers and his head fell back, his eyes closed as a long moan escaped from between his clenched teeth. He took a deep breath then grabbed her hand, stopping her as he opened his eyes and looked down at her.

"Angie, now. I can't wait."

She shuddered at the desperate need so clear in his eyes, so clear in his choked words. He shifted and yanked at his pants, tugging them down his hips until his erection stood completely free, hard, thick, long.

She twisted and bent over, closing her mouth around him, her tongue swirling along the smooth tip. He groaned and dug his fingers into her hair, holding her head in his lap as his hips thrust, pushing his cock deeper in her throat.

He groaned again then grabbed her, dragging her further across the console and into his lap, helping her move until she straddled him. Her knee banged against the steering wheel and his head hit the side of the door frame.

"Shit. Dammit. Hold on."

He reached around her and she could feel him fumbling with the keys, heard the electrical beep as he turned the key in the ignition. He reached down to the side, did something so the seat slid back, then he turned the key off, throwing them into darkness once more.

His hands closed around her hips and settled her more fully in his lap. She rocked her hips against him, rubbing against the length of his cock as he reached between them. His finger found her clit and stroked her, his touch sure, demanding.

His mouth crashed against hers again and she leaned into him. His skin was hot, feverish beneath her hungry touch, and she wanted more. Needed more.

She shifted her hips, searching, felt the tip of his cock poised at the entrance of her wet heat. But when she shifted once more, ready to impale herself on him, he grabbed her hips and held them steady.

He pulled back and watched her, his breathing rough, harsh.

"Fuck. Angie. I don't have any condoms."

"I'm on the pill."

Something flared in the depths of his eyes, hot and primitive. He grabbed her hips and drove himself into her, hard, deep. Her head dropped back with a harsh moan as he filled her.

Deeper. Harder.

Her hips moved, meeting each of his thrusts, answering his demands with her own. Over and over.

Harder. Faster.

She dug her hands into his shoulder as she rode him, his cock filling her, her slick wetness covering him. Need coiled inside her, alive, desperate. Building, tightening, demanding. Breathy moans filled the air, his and hers, as he drove into her. Over and over. Harder. Faster.

She tightened around him, desperation clawing at her as he filled her. Her head fell back on a small scream as her climax tore through her. Explosion after explosion rocked her, white heat searing her as lights danced behind her eyes.

His hands tightened on her hips, his thrusts becoming harder, more demanding. His fingers dug into her flesh as he drove into her. Once. Twice.

Once more as he growled her name in hunger.

His release filled her with liquid fire, pushing her back to the edge, pulling her over with him.

"Angie, God." He cupped her hands around her face and claimed her mouth once more. The kiss was deep and harsh, then slowed, becoming tender and sweet as their bodies slowly relaxed together. He pulled his mouth from hers and dropped kisses along her face, his breath warm against her moist skin.

"It's not enough, never enough. God, Angie, I can't enough of you. Never enough." His chest heaved against hers, his words sending chills of excitement through her. His arms tightened around her, pulling her even closer as he rested his head against her chest. She dropped her cheek to the top of his head as they held each other.

Minutes went by, second by second as her breathing returned to normal, as she slowly became aware of the world around them.

The soft stroke of Jay's hands against her back.

The crisp mountain air coming into the truck on a soft breeze.

The soft cricket song whispering in the forest around them.

A nagging cramp in her right leg, wedged against the door. She shifted, moaning at the sudden loss of Jay, then grabbed her leg.

Jay's shoulders started shaking under her and she pulled back, looking down at him in amusement. "Not funny."

He smiled, still chuckling, then pressed a quick kiss against her chest before easing her to the side. She slid back over the console, rubbing the cramp in her leg as she stretched.

She noticed Jay was doing the same. A small grimace crossed his face when he shifted in the seat then reached down beside him, moving the buckle for the seat belt out from under him. He muttered something under his breath, then pulled his sweatpants up past his hips with a grimace.

"I'm probably going to have a bruise on my ass tomorrow from that." He looked over at her, his eyes bright. "It'll definitely be worth it."

Angie laughed and leaned over, grabbing her clothes from the floor and getting dressed. She had just pulled her shirt on when Jay grabbed her arm and pulled her closer, kissing her.

He pulled away and ran his fingers through her hair, tucking one strand behind her ear. "Angie, when we get back—"

"I know. But let me handle Dave, okay?"

His gaze held hers, intent, serious. Searching. The air shifted around them, turning warm with anticipation once more. He opened his mouth, then closed it again and shook his head before leaning back.

"Okay, I'll try." He started the engine, turned on the headlights, put the truck in gear. Angie watched him, certain that he had been ready to say something else but had changed his mind at the last minute. But she didn't say anything, didn't question him.

And then they were back at the campsite, pulling in next to Mike's Jeep. Angie's eyes scanned the darkness around the campfire, searching for Dave among the faces sitting around the fire, joking, laughing, or just relaxing. But she didn't see him.

Jay reached out and squeezed her hand, and she noticed him looking off to the side. There, standing next to his truck, away from everyone else, stood Dave. She could make out his features in the reflection of the fire, noticed his clenched jaw and steely gaze watching them.

Her stomach gave a sickening lurch at the expression on his face.

"Angie, let me talk to him."

"No." She turned to Jay, tried to smile, then looked back at her brother. "No, this is something I need to."

She reached for the door handle but Jay pulled

her back, giving her a quick kiss and squeezing her hand once more. "Okay, but I'll be right over there."

She nodded her thanks then climbed out of the truck, closing the door behind her. Dave's gaze moved behind her, and she knew from the muscle that jumped in his tightened jaw that he was watching Jay. Just like she knew, without looking, that Jay watched him back.

Then Dave turned back to face her, his expression hard as she closed the distance between them. Chills danced across her skin and she folded her arms in front of her, wishing she had a jacket.

"Where have you been?" Dave's voice was pitched low so only she could hear. His words were clipped, his tone flat.

"We went out to dinner. I didn't realize I needed your permission."

"What's going on, Angie? I thought you broke things off with him?"

Frustration and hurt flared in her when she realized that he wouldn't even say Jay's name. And she didn't understand, didn't know why her beloved big brother was suddenly acting like a complete stranger.

"I changed my mind."

"Then change it back. I told you, I don't want you with him."

"It's not up to you, Dave. It never was. This is my life, not yours. You have to stop trying to run it!"

"I'm not trying to run it. I'm trying to protect you."

"No, you're not. You have to let me make my own decisions, you have to respect my choices."

"Respect?" He leaned closer, his voice humming

with contained fury, and something else, something she didn't understand. "Like you respect me when I tell you something?"

"No Dave, you don't tell. You don't advise. You demand or try to control, and you can't do that anymore, Dave." She took a deep breath, trying to steady her voice. "I don't understand, Dave. You never used to be like this. Why? What's going on? Why have you changed so much?"

He stepped back like she had slapped him, fire snapping in his eyes. The muscle in his jaw jumped, his teeth grinding together. He stared at her for a long second then shook his head.

"Pack your stuff, we're leaving."

"What? Are you insane? We're not leaving!"

"Yes, we are. Now let's go."

"I'm not leaving, Dave."

"I said—"

"I don't care what you said, I'm not leaving. I love him Dave, okay? You can either deal with it or not, but you're not going to tell me what to do anymore."

The words shocked her, nearly as much as they obviously shocked him. Where had they come from? And did she mean them?

She closed her eyes, needing to block the look of condemnation in her brother's eyes as she thought, listened, felt. A sense of something peaceful and warm, something right, filled her.

She loved Jay.

She didn't care if it was too soon, didn't care right now if the emotion was returned, she only knew that it was right.

She opened her eyes to see Dave watching her,

his jaw still clenched, his eyes filled with anger and hurt. She reached out to touch his arm but he brushed her hand away and stepped back.

Pain sliced through her and she blinked back the sudden tears building behind her eyes. "Dave?"

"No, Angela. You know how I feel. Don't expect me to approve or condone." His words were cold and empty, aimed at her heart whether he intended that or not. She blinked again, wanting to reach out to him but afraid he'd brush her off once more. Then he looked away and pushed past her, saying nothing more as he headed toward the darkness of the woods, away from the campfire and everyone there.

She watched him disappear, his body swallowed by the night. Long minutes went by as she stared into the darkness, torn between going after him.

Or letting him go.

But what could she say that hadn't already been said? What else could she do? Because she wouldn't do the one thing he asked—demanded—of her. She was through living her life for anyone else. Including her brother.

She wiped a hand across her eyes and took a deep breath, then headed back to the campfire. Jay watched her, his eyes questioning. His shoulders slumped when she shook her head and he patted the empty chair next to his. She walked over and sat down, accepting the wine cooler he held out for her.

He leaned over and grabbed her hand, lacing his fingers with hers then bringing their combined hands to his mouth. He dropped a kiss along her knuckles, then held their hands in his lap.

Just held them, offering her his warmth, his strength, his comfort.

PLAYING WITH FIRE

Chapter Twenty-Five

Dave left in the middle of the night.

Angie stood in front of the fire, wrapped in Jay's sweatshirt, her hands folded around a mug of coffee. And she was still cold, a slab of ice lodged deep in her stomach, chilling her from the inside.

She glanced across the campsite, seeing the empty spot where his tent had been last night. Her eyes drifted over to the vehicles parked further away, searching for his truck even though she knew it was gone. Looking for it again wouldn't make it suddenly reappear.

Dave had actually left. Packed up his things and left. Without saying anything to anyone.

And leaving her behind.

That was the part that bothered her the most, that he could just leave her. He had been upset with her last night, angry. But she didn't understand what she had done so wrong to make him actually leave her behind. Without a single word.

She raised the mug to her lips and choked down

a swallow of coffee, forcing it down her swollen throat. The brew was strong and bitter, even with the added cream and sugar, but it was hot and she needed that, needed it to dispel the iciness inside her.

Arms wrapped around her waist from behind and she momentarily stiffened, surprised, then leaned back against Jay's broad chest. He kissed her cheek and held her in silence as people milled around the campsite behind them.

Everyone's initial shock at Dave's departure had worn off, everyone but hers, but she knew a few of them were still talking about it. Part of her wondered if they blamed her, if they thought it was her fault that he had left. She didn't think they did, not unless their comments and musings had solely been for her benefit.

No. They had been as genuinely surprised as she.

"We can leave now if you want."

She placed her hand over Jay's and squeezed, grateful for the offer. But she shook her head. "No, I don't want to leave. I just wish I knew why—"

"I know. I do, too." His arms tightened, briefly, then he stepped back. She turned and looked up at him; her heart skipped a little at the look in his eyes. Warmth, worry, concern. Damn Dave for pulling this stunt. Damn him for thinking only of himself.

What did he honestly think would happen if he left? Was he trying to teach her a lesson? Send her a message? That's what confused her the most: what he hoped to accomplish by leaving.

"C'mon. Breakfast is ready, you need to eat something."

They walked over to the cooking area, where Pete and Jimmy were arguing over how crispy the bacon should be before they took it off the griddle. Jay grabbed two paper plates and handed one to Angie, then pushed the quarreling chefs out of the way so they could get their food.

"See. Crispy. Everyone likes it crispy!" Pete waved a pair of tongs toward Jimmy, then pointed at Angie's plate as proof. She laughed then, just because she could, grabbed two slices of the less-crispy bacon before scooping up some scrambled eggs.

"Guess she showed you, huh?" Jimmy reached around and started pulling bacon from the griddle and placing it on a larger platter.

"You're breaking my heart, Angie. Just breaking my heart."

Jay smacked Pete in the stomach as he walked by, causing the man to grunt in mock pain. Angie laughed, then walked with Jay over to the table to join Mike and Nick. Mike looked up at her and gave her a small smile.

"You okay?"

"Yeah. Just...surprised, I guess. When I talked to him last night, he was angry and told me to pack up and leave. I told him no. But I still can't believe that he just left." Angie nibbled at a piece of bacon, noticing the look that Jay and Mike exchanged. She didn't say anything, just looked at both of them and waited.

"Angie, has anything happened in the last few months, anything at all that maybe—" Mike paused, glanced at Jay, then shrugged. "Is there something else that could be going on? Because I just don't buy him being this upset over you two seeing each other."

Angie finished the bacon then shook her head. "Nothing that I know of. And believe me, I've been trying to think of anything. He got upset with me a couple months ago about working too much at the bar, said I was going to burn myself out, but he hasn't been crazy about me working there since I started."

"Jay, I know you don't want to hear this but, maybe you should talk to him tomorrow when you take Angie home."

"Yeah, I was already planning on it. I have a few things I'd like to tell him."

Angie reached out and put her hand on Jay's arm, shaking her head.

"Jay, no. That's only going to make things worse."

Mike shook her head as well, frowning at Jay. "Jay, I don't mean tell him off. I mean *talk* to him. Maybe you can figure out what's going on. Because this isn't like him."

Jay stared across the table, giving Mike an unreadable look, then blew out his breath and finally nodded. "Fine. But as soon as he starts something, I'm done."

Mike ignored him then looked back at Angie. "In the meantime, if things get that bad and you need a place to stay, my old place is open. You're more than welcome to stay there as long as you want. It's even furnished." There was a soft thud from under the table and Mike suddenly jumped, her hand reaching under the table. She fixed Jay with an annoyed look. "What the hell was that for?"

Jay's eyes widened in innocence. "What? I don't know what you're talking about."

Angie watched the byplay in curiosity, knowing she was missing something, but having no idea what it was. She looked over at Nick, who was trying to smother a laugh. And not very successfully.

She decided to ignore all of it and thanked Mike for the offer. "I appreciate it but I have one more year of school left—and the tuition to go with it. The scholarship helps with some, but not all of it. And while Grant pays me a decent amount, not to mention the tips, that's not enough to cover rent on top of everything else."

"No rent. And utilities are included in that, too. Unless you wanted something besides basic cable."

Angie stared at Mike in open-mouth shock, unable to believe what she was hearing. Was the woman actually offering her a place to stay, completely rent-free? But why?

"Don't read too much into it, Angie." Nick explained. "Kayla's referring to her apartment, which is actually a renovated barn on her dad's property. She doesn't live there anymore and her dad has no interest in renting it out. He keeps hoping that she'll leave me and move back home. It's a nice place, so just let us know if you're interested."

"Wow. Uh, thanks. I'm not sure what to say."

"No need to say anything." Mike waved away her thanks. "Just know that you've got a place to stay if you need it."

"Or she can just stay with me, you know."

Silence greeted Jay's sudden outburst, but only for a few seconds before Mike started laughing. Even Nick chuckled. But Angie didn't know how to react, or what to even say. She turned to see Jay watching her, one corner of his mouth tilted in a slight grin. More surprising than his offer was the faint blush that colored his cheeks, the pink growing slightly darker as she watched him.

"I mean, you don't have to worry. If something happens, or if you just need to get away, you have a place to stay." Jay's voice was steady but the blush on his face darkened, and she wondered if she was reading too much into it or not.

Wondering if she wanted to read too much into it.

And she still didn't know what to say. She shifted on the hard bench and looked down at her lap, then at her nearly empty plate, then finally back at Jay. "Okay. Thanks. I, uh, appreciate that. All of you."

Jay finally looked away and Mike and Nick laughed again, confusing Angie even more. She watched as Mike wadded up a napkin and tossed it at Jay, hitting him square in the chest.

"You're smooth, Jay. Real smooth."

And again, Angie couldn't help but feel like she was missing something.

Chapter Twenty-Six

Jay reached up and pulled his sunglasses off then tossed them on the dashboard. The sun had started sinking behind them and he didn't need them anymore.

What he needed was some magic wand or pill or something, anything, to use to make Angie smile. A real smile, not just an attempt at a half smile. The first few hours had been fine, with easy conversation and bantering that made the miles fly by. Too quickly, for his tastes. But there were still moments when she turned quiet and he knew without asking that she was thinking of Dave and the stunt he had pulled Tuesday night.

It was a dick move, and he had every intention of telling him that. Not that he'd said that much to Angie, though he was pretty sure she knew his exact thoughts on the entire matter.

So while she had been quiet, he hadn't worried too much, not when he knew how upset the whole situation had made her. But she had grown increasingly quieter during the last hour and he didn't know what to say, didn't know how to reassure her.

Even if he could reassure her.

They were only about ten minutes from her house and the tension coming off her now was nearly suffocating. And he hated seeing her like this, hated knowing that he was, at least in part, to blame.

From Dave's perspective anyway.

Jay sighed and stretched his back, feeling a small pop at the base of his spine. He looked over at Angie and felt a surge of warmth unfurl beneath his breastbone. She was staring out the window, pensive, her shoulders slightly hunched around her ears.

And he would do anything, anything at all, to make her pain go away.

He reached across the console and took her hand in his, gently squeezing. She turned in the seat and offered him a shadow of a smile, then gazed back out the window.

"Angie, what I said yesterday morning, about staying with me. I was serious. You don't have to go home." He tried to find the right tone, something between comforting and caring, trying not to sound like he was asking her to move in. He wasn't sure how successful he was, because he suddenly realized he would love nothing more than waking up beside her each morning.

And what kind of an ass was he, hoping she could read between the lines when she didn't even know how he felt? When she was worried about this whole situation with Dave?

And he wished he could take the words back, because surely she'd think he was crazy, but it was too late. She looked over at him and smiled, another ghost smile, and squeezed his hand.

"I know, thanks. That actually means a lot."

Jay nodded then turned his attention back to the road, not knowing if he should be relieved—or disappointed. And then it didn't matter because he was turning into the development where she lived. She stiffened in the seat next to him and he realized she was even more worried than he thought.

He turned into the driveway and parked behind Dave's truck, shut off the engine, then turned in his seat. "Do you want me to go in and talk to him first?"

A split-second of relief crossed her face and Jay was certain she was going to say yes. Then she frowned and shook her head. "No, but thanks." Before he could say anything else, she opened the door and climbed out.

He followed, walking around to the back and grabbing her gear. She reached for her duffel bag and Jay held it out for her, ready to hand it to her.

But he couldn't, not yet, not when she looked so uncertain.

He dropped the bag to the ground and pulled her into his arms, pressing what he hoped was a comforting kiss against her lips. He cupped her face in both hands and tilted her head up so she was looking at him. His eyes searched hers, quiet, intent.

"Angie, I just want you to know..." His voice trailed off, his heart hammering so loud in his chest he was surprised she couldn't hear it. He cleared his throat and ran his tongue across his suddenly dry lips, searching for the words that shouldn't be so hard to find. He closed his eyes and took a deep breath, then opened them to see Angie watching him in curiosity.

"Angie, whatever happens, I just...Oh hell." He

closed his mouth over hers, intent, demanding. His tongue swept into her mouth, tasting. She moaned, a bare whisper of breath mingling with his as she leaned in closer. He pulled his mouth away, stared down into her dazed eyes. "I love you."

Her eyes widened, then she blinked. And blinked again, her gaze stunned. The bottom of Jay's stomach dropped and he closed his eyes. God, he was a freaking idiot. Why couldn't he have just kept his mouth shut? He gently released his hold on her face and stepped back, wondering if he should apologize, wondering if he should say something else. But he didn't get a chance because Angie was suddenly pressed against him, her lips warm against his as she kissed him, long and hard.

He opened his eyes and looked down, felt the coldness in his belly disappear as she watched him with wide eyes. "I love you, Jay." She wrapped her arms around him and kissed him again, slow, hot, welcoming.

His arms closed around her, holding her even closer as he lost himself in her touch, in her warmth. Awareness flashed in the back of his mind, reminding him where they were, what he had to do, and he gentled the kiss, finally pulling away.

He smiled down at her and reached out to tuck a strand of hair behind her ear. "Just remember that when we go in there, okay? I'm here for you, Angie, no matter what."

She nodded, but neither one of them moved. It was as if they were afraid to, afraid some spell might be broken if they did. But Jay knew they couldn't stay here all night, couldn't put off whatever else might happen, so he gave her one more quick kiss then leaned down and grabbed her duffel bag.

She watched him, chewing on her lower lip in indecision, then nodded once more. She grabbed the other bag then turned away and headed toward the house, Jay right behind her.

The living room was empty and quiet, the television against the far wall turned on but with the sound muted. Jay looked around, his gaze wary, not knowing what to expect.

Not really knowing what he had expected. Maybe Dave waiting for him with a shotgun?

Yeah, that was an exaggeration. Probably. But tension still hummed inside, tight, cautious, his anticipation making him edgy. He dropped Angie's bag next to the stairs then waited.

"Dave? I'm home." Angie called out, dropping her other bag next to the first one. She cocked her head, listening, then moved off toward the back of the house, toward the kitchen. That's when Jay noticed it, the sound of running water and the clatter of pans.

He followed Angie into the kitchen just as Dave turned from the stove. His eyes rested first on Angie, then moved to Jay. His gaze was hard, intense, unwelcoming. He turned back to the stove, his attention on whatever he was cooking. A minute went by before he moved the pan and placed it on the counter, then turned back to face them.

"You know, an apology might be nice." Anger laced Angie's words but Jay could hear the hurt under them. He wondered if Dave could, as well. If he did, he didn't acknowledge it, just fixed his sister with that cool detached expression, one brow raised in question.

"Apology for what?"

"For what? Are you serious? How about for just taking off like that, without a word to anyone? How about for just leaving me behind with no way home?"

Dave crossed his arms and watched Angie for another second, then looked pointedly at Jay before turning back to her. "Doesn't look like you had any trouble finding a way home to me."

"Why are you being like this, Dave? What the hell have I done to so seriously piss you off?" Angie was shouting now, whatever hurt and anger that had been buried inside her the last two days bubbling to the surface. Jay shifted his weight from one foot to the other, wondering how far he should let her go—should let them both go.

Because even though Dave hadn't moved, Jay knew the man's anger was also simmering just under the surface. And he didn't know if this would just be an argument between siblings, or if it would explode into something else.

"We've already had this discussion, Angie. I'm not repeating myself."

"No! No, we haven't. There hasn't been any discussion! There's just been you, demanding and commanding and getting pissed off! And I don't know why, and I can't handle it anymore!" Angie's voice broke with her final words and Jay wanted to go over to her, to wrap his arms around her and comfort her and tell her everything would be alright. But he watched Dave, saw the muscle jump in his clenched jaw. His dark eyes betrayed no emotion as he watched Angie.

Then there was a sudden flash of something, noticeable only because Jay was watching so carefully.

And Jay knew what was coming, stepped forward to hold his hand out to Dave. To stop him from speaking, stop him from saying something he couldn't take back.

But he was too late, because the words were already out, loud and clear.

"You're free to live elsewhere if you feel you can't handle it."

"Dammit." Jay turned away from Dave and moved to Angie's side, worried only about her. Color drained from her face as she stared at her brother, shock and surprise clear in her wide dark eyes, so much like her brother's.

Jay wrapped an arm around her shoulder, tried to turn her so she was facing him. But her body was stiff, immobile, as she kept staring at Dave.

"Angie, c'mon, let's go into the other room, let me talk to him—"

She shook her head, a strand of hair falling into her wide eyes. Then she blinked and took a deep breath, and raised her chin a notch before facing Jay.

"Can I crash at your place tonight?" Her voice was even, a little cold. Jay glanced over at Dave, then back at her and nodded.

"Of course. You know that."

She nodded, and Jay noticed the fine trembling of her lips before she tightened her mouth. She tossed one last look at Dave then walked out of the kitchen.

Jay watched her disappear then turned back to Dave, his own anger rushing to the surface. Heavy silence descended on them, long seconds passing with each tick of the clock on the wall.

"Why the hell are you treating your sister like this? What is going on with you?" Jay was surprised at how calm his voice was, how steady. Dave looked over at him and met his gaze, watching, studying, before looking away.

And in that brief second of time, Jay saw something he didn't know how to interpret. Something that looked like regret—mixed with relief.

Then he wondered if he imagined it, because Dave's voice was just as cool and steady as it had been earlier.

"That doesn't really concern you, does it?"

"Yeah, I think it does." Jay watched him, searching for any sign of the emotion he had thought he'd seen, then shook his head. "Dave, what's going on? We've been friends for too long for you to be acting like this. And I can't believe that you're so set against us seeing each other that you'd take it out on Angie like this."

But Dave didn't bother replying, wouldn't even look at Jay anymore. He turned away and busied himself at the stove, moving more pans and making so much noise that Jay stepped closer to hear, just in case he did say something.

"Dammit Dave, say something! Do you honestly think I'd hurt her? I love her!"

Dave's back stiffened. Jay watched in shock as he threw a pan into the sink. Food splattered along the wall and onto the floor, but Dave made no move to clean it up. Instead, he stood there, his back to Jay, his hands braced, white-knuckled, against the edge of the counter.

Silence fell over them again, even more oppressive. Dave's breaths were harsh, tension clear in the rigid set to his shoulders. Jay didn't know what else to say, what else to do. He stood there, waiting, then let out his breath and turned to walk out of the kitchen.

"It's not you."

Jay paused then turned back. But Dave was still facing the wall, the muscles in his arms bulging from the grip he maintained on the counter. "Then what is it? Talk to me, Dave, tell me what's going on."

But Dave didn't answer, barely even shook his head in response. Jay heard Angie's footsteps on the stairs, knew he had only seconds. "Dave?"

But the man in front of him just shook his head again, saying nothing. Jay sighed, not knowing what else to do, then turned to walk out of the kitchen. Dave's voice stopped him.

"You keep her safe, or I *will* come after you."

Jay turned to see Dave staring after him, his look serious, dangerous. And there was something else, something Jay thought he must be imagining. But Dave turned back around and started cleaning up the mess he had made. It was clear he wasn't going to say anything else.

Jay walked away, his confusion even greater now that it had been earlier. Angie waited for him by the front door, a backpack slung over her shoulder and a large duffel bag in her hand. Her eyes were red, shock still clear on her face.

And Jay forgot about Dave, forgot about that look of relief and gratitude in his eyes, and focused on what was most important: Angie.

He grabbed the small duffel bag he had placed near the stairs, then followed Angie out the door, pulling it closed behind him. He helped place the bags in her car, then pulled her into his arms for a brief hug.

"You sure about this?"

She nodded, then tilted her head back to look at him. "Yeah. I just need to get out of here for a while."

Jay nodded and pressed his lips to hers, then walked to his truck as she got into her car.

And he thought again about the look of gratitude in Dave's eyes.

Chapter Twenty-Seven

A slight breeze blew through the open windows, stirring the hot humid air that hovered over everything. Two fans were set up, one inside the living room, one inside the kitchen. Right now, the only thing they were doing was moving the hot air from one end of the downstairs to the other.

Angie pushed the box she had been digging through to the side then sat back on her heels and looked around. The apartment was nice. Much nicer than she had imagined it would be when Mike had told her it was actually a renovated barn.

And for now, it was hers.

Kind of.

She hadn't been willing to accept Mike's offer of free rent, no matter how much the woman insisted. So they had come to an agreement that made them both happy. Well, one that made Angie happy. She honestly didn't think Mike cared one way or the other, and thought the only reason she finally agreed to it was because of Jay.

Angie smiled at the memory. He hadn't been thrilled about her moving in here, not when he had been hoping she'd agree to move in with him. But as soon as he realized she wasn't going to change her mind, he badgered Mike until she finally agreed to the idea of accepting rent from Angie.

Yes, her budget was going to be a little tight for the next few months, but it was doable.

Not that she hadn't thought about accepting Jay's offer. She had. Repeatedly. The thought of waking in his arms each morning, the thought of just being with him, was almost too much temptation to resist.

But it was too soon.

Too much, too soon, given that she still wasn't speaking with Dave. A week had gone by since they came back from the camping trip and he still wouldn't answer her calls, wouldn't return her messages.

Angie pushed the hair out of her face then reached behind her and tightened the scrunchie around her ponytail. She needed to push thoughts of her brother from her mind, at least for now. She still didn't understand what had happened, why he was acting like this.

But she had resolved not to let that run her life. She couldn't, not if she wanted to be happy. And part of her was convinced that, no matter what else was going on, Dave would want her to be happy. How many times had he said those exact words to her?

So she had to believe them, and trust that everything else would eventually work itself out. It had to.

"Holy shit, it's like an oven in here. You do know this place has air conditioning, right?" Jay pushed through the front door with another box, sweat turning his hair darker. He dropped the box to the floor then pulled the hem of his t-shirt up to wipe at his face, giving Angie a very nice view of his sculpted stomach.

"You like that, huh?"

Angie blinked then looked up to see Jay grinning down at her. She also noticed that he didn't bother lowering his shirt, at least not right away. She pushed to her feet with a small groan then walked over to him, her finger trailing a line from his chest down to the waistband of his low-slung gym shorts.

"Hmm. Maybe. I might need to see it up close before I can decide." She leaned in closer and kissed him, sighing when his arms wrapped around her and held her tight against him.

He pulled away much too soon and smiled down at her. "I love you."

"I love you too." She leaned up, ready for another kiss, but he stepped back.

"No, I'm disgusting and all sweaty."

She wiggled her brows at him and smiled. "Maybe I like it all sweaty."

"Oh God, you're killing me." He grabbed her by the shoulders and pulled her closer, dropping a quick, hard kiss on her lips before stepping back. "But I need a shower. And why don't you have the air conditioning on?"

"It's on upstairs."

"Angie, nobody is going to say anything about you running the AC upstairs and downstairs at the same time. Trust me."

"Yeah, I know, but it's still…I don't know. Weird, I guess. I didn't want to take advantage."

"You're not, so stop worrying." Jay walked into

the kitchen and opened the refrigerator, digging around until he pulled out two bottles of water. He handed one to her, then twisted the top off his and gulped it down in several long swallows.

"Thirsty?"

"Scorched." He tossed the bottle into the recycling bin then leaned against the counter, watching her for a few seconds. "So what do you think so far?"

"About?"

"Your new place. Moving. All of it. I know it's a change for you."

Angie looked around, taking everything in again. Spacious kitchen, informal dining room, cozy living room. And already furnished, which was an added bonus.

Good thing, too, since she didn't have much in the way of furniture except for her bedroom set. Jay and Nick had brought that over earlier and set it up already. In fact, except for the box of books she had been sorting through and the box of mementos Jay had just brought in, she was pretty much moved in already.

It was exciting. Yet a little sad, too.

She turned back to Jay and smiled. "I think I'm going to like it."

"Yeah? Good." He watched her for another second, one corner of his mouth lifted in a grin. "Even if it is an oven in here."

She laughed then gave in and started closing the windows. Jay wasted no time and went straight to thermostat to turn on the air conditioning. She heard it kick in and a minute later felt cool air blowing from the vents. She went into the living room and turned the fan off, then looked back at Jay. His eyes travelled the length of her body, warming her, before meeting her gaze.

"So. Were you planning on sleeping here tonight?"

"Well, it is kind of my new apartment." A look of disappointment crossed his face and she had to bite the inside of her cheek to keep from smiling.

"Yeah, it is." He cleared his throat and gave her another look, his gray eyes darkening with desire. She smiled then walked over to the stairs, looking back over her shoulder at him.

"Yes. It is."

"Where are you going?"

"Me?" She shrugged and kept climbing the stairs, tossing one more look over her shoulder to see if he was following. She smiled when she saw he was only a few steps behind her. "I was just thinking that you were right, it is hot."

"Yeah?"

"Yeah. And I feel a little grungy myself. I thought I'd take a shower."

"Is that so?"

Angie turned around and walked backward, toward the bathroom. She grabbed the hem of her shirt and pulled it over her head, tossing it on the bed as she walked by. Her sports bra followed. She stopped in the doorway of the bathroom and shimmied out of her shorts, kicking them away from her.

She braced one arm on the doorframe, standing in nothing but a lace thong. Jay stopped a few feet away, his gaze drinking her in. Her eyes roamed down his body, staring pointedly at the erection clearly visible under his gym shorts. Then she looked up at him and smiled, wet heat already pooling between her legs.

"Have you seen this shower? It's huge. And it has a Jacuzzi tub."

"Uh, yeah." Jay cleared his throat. "Yeah, I have seen it."

Angie hooked her thumbs into the waist band of the thong and eased the scrap of lace down past her thighs. She kept her eyes on his, reveling in the passion, in the love, so clear in their gray depths. Then she bent over and stepped out of her underwear, twirling the lace around her finger as she straightened.

And threw them straight at Jay.

"I was kind of hoping you'd help me break it in."

His throat moved in a long swallow and his eyes darkened even more.

"You know you're playing with fire, right?"

She shrugged and smiled. "Then I guess it's a good thing you're a firefighter, isn't it?"

He watched her, grinning, as she backed into the bathroom. Less than three seconds later, he was naked in front of her, his arms wrapped around her waist and his mouth pressed hard against hers. He pulled back and smiled.

"I guess that's a damn good thing."

Epilogue

Dave walked down the hall and stopped at the door of Angie's room. The curtains hung limp at the window, the drawn shades keeping the room in shadow. Not that there was anything to see. His sister had packed up, moved out.

Jay and Nick had come by today, taking the bed and nightstands and lamps.

The room was empty now, as empty of spirit as it was of furnishings.

There was nothing left except a few framed posters and the large corkboard that had been hanging along the far wall of the room for as long as he could remember.

He stepped into the room and walked over to the corkboard, trying to tell himself he wasn't intruding, he wasn't spying. Angie didn't live here, there was nothing to spy on.

Tightness squeezed his chest as his gaze rested on a picture tacked in the corner of the corkboard. The picture had been taken just over two years ago, the day he had come back home after spending eighteen months in hell. He was in uniform, his arm draped over Angie's shoulder as she leaned into him, one arm wrapped around his waist, a small Flag waving in her hand as they both smiled into the camera.

Dave reached out and touched the picture with one finger, swallowing against the emotion clogging his throat. His eyes drifted to the note pinned next to the picture and he frowned. The scrap of paper was new, only recently placed there, Angie's sloppy chicken-scratch writing scrawled across it in black ink.

You're always going to be my big brother. Love you back.

Dave dropped his hand and stared at the note, wondering when she had put it there, wondering how she knew he'd even see it.

He shook his head then reached into his pocket and grabbed his phone, anger and fear surging through him as he re-read the text message.

I know what you did. You'll pay.

Yes, he'd always be Angie's big brother, which meant protecting her—even if that meant pushing her away.

Dave turned and walked out of the room, closing the door behind him.

*****

ABOUT THE AUTHOR

Lisa B. Kamps is the author of the best-selling series The Baltimore Banners, featuring "hard-hitting, heart-melting hockey players", on and off the ice. PLAYING WITH FIRE is the second title of her anticipated new series, *Firehouse Fourteen*, featuring hot and heroic firefighters.

Lisa has always loved writing, even during her assorted careers: first as a firefighter with the Baltimore County Fire Department, then a very brief (and not very successful) stint at bartending in east Baltimore, and finally as the Director of Retail Operations for a busy Civil War non-profit.

Lisa currently lives in Maryland with her husband and two sons, one very spoiled Border Collie, two cats with major attitude, several head of cattle, and entirely too many chickens to count.

Interested in reaching out to Lisa? She'd love to hear from you, and there are several ways to contact her:

Website: www.LisaBKamps.com
Newsletter: www.lisabkamps.com/signup/
Email: LisaBKamps@gmail.com
Facebook: www.facebook.com/authorLisaBKamps
Twitter: twitter.com/LBKamps
Goodreads: www.goodreads.com/LBKamps
Instagram: www.instagram.com/lbkamps/

Lisa B. Kamps

BREAKING PROTOCOL
Firehouse Fourteen Book 3

Dave Warren knows all about protocol. As a firefighter/paramedic, he has to. What he doesn't know is when his life became nothing more than routine, following the rules day in and day out. Has it always been that way or was it a gradual change? Did it have anything to do with his time spent overseas as a medic with the Army Reserves? He's not sure, but it's something he's learned to accept and live with—until a series of messages upsets his routine. And until one spitfire Flight Medic enters his life.

Carolann "CC" Covey has no patience for protocols. Yes, they're a necessary evil, a part of her job, but they don't rule her life. She can't let them—she knows life is for the living, a lesson learned the hard way overseas. Which is why her attraction to the serious and staid Dave Warren makes no sense. Is it just a case of "opposites attract", or is it something more? Will CC be able to teach him that sometimes rules need to be broken?

And when something sinister appears from Dave's past to threaten everything he's come to love, will he learn that Breaking Protocol may be the only way to save what's really important?

Turn the page for an exciting sneak peek at BREAKING PROTOCOL.

CC rapped her knuckles against the door for the second time, wondering if anyone was home, or if she was just wasting her time. A truck sat in the driveway, an impressive full-size extended cab heavy duty job. Shiny black paint, shiny chrome. The truck fit the owner, she thought.

If it actually belonged to Big Guy.

She stepped back from the door and looked around. The neighborhood was quiet, the homes on the upper end of modest and nicely maintained. The lawn that spread out around her was neatly clipped and edged, the flower beds that lined the walk from the driveway filled with blooming bushes and a selection of vibrantly colored flowers. She had no idea what kind of flowers, knew only that they looked nice.

She glanced at her watch. It wasn't quite ten o'clock in the morning. Maybe the Big Guy was in the shower. Or maybe he wasn't even home.

Or maybe he was sleeping.

CC smiled at the clear visual that sprung to mind, immediately figuring him for a guy who slept in the buff. And wouldn't that be a nice little treat, if he answered the door like that?

Figuring the third time was a charm, she opened the screen once more and rapped her knuckles against the thick wood door. Harder this time, just in case.

Maybe a little too hard, since she could hear muffled grumbling coming from the other side. The door finally opened, only about six inches, but wide enough for her to realize that the Big Guy had, indeed, been sleeping.

Unfortunately, not in the buff.

But damn close to it.

Her eyes raked over his body in slow appreciation, from his sleep-mussed black hair and piercing chocolate eyes, down to his broad well-defined chest. And wasn't she the lucky one, because that chest was deliciously bare. Her eyes continued their slow descent, down past his sculpted abs and lean hips—damn shame he was wearing such baggy shorts—to his strong legs and bare feet.

Her eyes reversed their travel, pausing to study the intricately drawn tattoo on his left chest, and came back to rest on his dark eyes. She didn't miss the scowl on his face, an expression that made him look just like a pirate, especially with the dark stubble that shadowed his strong chin and jaw.

"Can I help you?" His voice was gruff, hoarse with sleep. Not a single flicker of recognition showed in his eyes.

CC slid the sunglasses up to her head, anchoring them in her hair, and gave him a big smile.

"Hey Big Guy. Did I wake you?"

Recognition, and something very much like surprise, quickly registered on his face. He stepped back, but didn't open the door any wider or invite her in.

"You!"

"Yup, it's me. So, you going to invite me in?" She reached her hand out and nudged the door open a bit, her eyes quickly roaming around the shadowed interior. Neutral living room with a dining room just beyond, stairs leading up off to the right. "Or are you hiding a wife or girlfriend in here?"

He stepped back in mute surprise as she walked past him. He wasn't married—she had already checked on that—but she wasn't sure about the girlfriend part. She looked over her shoulder at him, not surprised that he hadn't moved.

"What?" His brows pulled down in an angry slash as he stared at her. "No! To all the above."

"Hey, just checking. Sometimes you can never tell."

"No." He shook his head, then turned back to the door and looked surprised that it was still standing open. He closed it, probably harder than he intended, then turned back to face her. He ran both hands across his face then up through his hair and exhaled deeply. "Is there a reason you're here?"

"Yeah. You left this in the chopper, thought you might want it back." She pulled his wallet from the back pocket of her jeans and tossed it to him. It hit him dead center in the chest and he reached up, fumbling to catch it before it hit the ground. He stared at it for a long second, then shook his head again.

"My wallet. Yeah, I know. I was going to run down later today to pick it up at the barracks."

"Lucky you. I just saved you a trip." She walked into the living room and looked around, her eyes noticing more details. Not that there was much to see.

A beige leather sofa and loveseat formed an L, allowing optimal viewing of the large screen television mounted to the far wall. Matching dark oak end tables flanked the sofa, complementing the dark oak coffee table placed conveniently in the middle of the arrangement. Boring. Really boring. A few pictures on the wall added some color, as did the area rug. Other than that, there wasn't much to see.

She moved through the living room to the dining room. A shaker style oak table with whitewashed legs was flanked by four ladder back chairs and a matching bench. An old fashioned hutch stood to the side, an assortment of dishes and collectibles stacked behind the glass doors.

The furniture and decoration wasn't bad, but she would have preferred some color herself.

"So. Do you have anything to drink around here, Big Guy?" He was right behind her, she could feel his presence less than a foot away, and she didn't have to turn around to know he was still scowling. She bit back her smile and wandered into the kitchen, knowing he was following her.

Now this was more like it, she thought. The kitchen was bright and airy, with big windows and French doors opening to the backyard. Yellows, greens and blues mixed in a vibrant color scheme, an extension of the outdoors contained just beyond the glass. She moved over to the counter island, hooked the heel of her boot around a stool, and pulled it out. She sat her elbows on the granite surface, propped her chin in her hands, and offered Big Guy a bright smile.

He was still scowling at her, confusion warring

with something else on his face. One hand reached up and he absently scratched at his chest, pulling her attention once again to the tattoo.

About five inches square, it was a detailed black ink drawing of a caduceus against a tattered Flag. The words "My Brother's Keeper" formed a border along the top and side. Even from this distance, she could see the detail was exquisite, and her fingers itched to trace the lines.

And not just of the tattoo.

"Nice ink. When'd you get it?"

"Excuse me?" He glanced down at his chest, then dropped his hand to the side, his fingers curling into a loose fist. She could feel his frustration from where she sat, and smiled even wider. "I'm sorry, but is there a reason you're here?"

"Just wanted to drop off your wallet."

"And you did, thank you. Now you can leave."

CC didn't flinch at his rudeness, not when she knew it was a result of his being flustered, by not knowing what to make of her. She almost laughed, but didn't think he'd appreciate it. "You can't even offer me a drink before I go? I'm not picky. Water's fine."

Big Guy watched her with narrowed eyes, his impatience and uncertainty warring with something else, something that caused just a brief flicker of heat to flash in his dark eyes. He muttered something then turned his back on her and reached up to grab a glass from a cabinet. Her eyes roamed across his broad shoulders and down his back, down to the tight ass that even his baggy shorts couldn't hide.

He turned on the faucet and let it run for a second, then placed the glass under the running water until it was filled. He brought the glass over and sat it in front of her with a small clink, his gaze still narrowed.

"No ice?"

Without a word, he turned to the steel-fronted refrigerator, opened the door, and reached into the ice bin. He returned and plunked two ice cubes into the glass, ignoring the water that splashed over the rim.

"Thank you." She smiled and raised the glass in a mock salute then took a long swallow, her eyes never leaving his. She lowered the glass and ran her tongue across her lips, noticing that his gaze dropped to her mouth, watching. Another flare of heat sparked in his eyes and he looked away.

"Now that you've dropped off my wallet—and had something to drink—you can leave."

"Are you always so grumpy, Big Guy?"

"Dave. The name is Dave." He uttered the words through clenched teeth, his frustration clear. "And when strangers show up at my house uninvited, yes, I get a little grumpy."

"Strangers, hm?" She took another swallow of water then put the glass down, pushing it out of her way. She folded her arms on the counter then leaned forward, watching him. "You know, something funny about that. I've learned that people who talk to one another, get to know each other, aren't strangers for very long."

Dave just watched her, saying nothing. She kept her eyes on his, refusing to look away. A small twitch teased the corner of his mouth, just the briefest movement, but she saw it. Saw it, and smiled.

His tension eased out of him, bit by bit until his shoulders weren't hunched quite so tightly against his ears. Lines eased from his face, relaxing his mouth and eyes and making him look younger, less worried, more approachable. CC felt a small glimmer of victory shoot through her at the transformation. She knew she hadn't read him wrong last night.

"That's really nice work, by the way." She nodded her head to the tattoo again. "When did you get it done?"

He looked down at his chest then up at her and shrugged. "About three years ago. Um, excuse me, I need to go grab a shirt—"

"No, really, you don't. I'm kind of enjoying the scenery." Her words stopped him cold and he froze mid-step, the tips of his ears turning pink. She watched the muscles in his strong throat work, and briefly wondered if he was trying to swallow—or trying not to choke. He didn't say anything but he did turn to look at her, now only a foot away from her.

She swiveled on the stool and leaned forward, reaching out and tracing the outline of the tattoo with the tip of her finger. The muscle underneath was rock hard, the flesh firm and hot, scorching. His chest rose and fell with one deep breath before his hand shot out and closed around her wrist.

She slid off the stool and stepped next to him, looking up into his eyes, watching heat swirl in their depths.

"What are you doing?" His voice was a hoarse whisper, tugging at something deep inside her. But there was something else, a wariness, a hunger, a deep need that pulsed through him and into her.

"So I'm not the only one who felt it." She breathed the words, barely aware of saying them out loud, wondering even as she said them what he was thinking.

What he would think if she leaned up and pressed her lips against the pulse beating heavily at the base of his throat? If she leaned up and pressed her lips against his mouth?

Anticipation, excitement, need. Heat. Desire. They swirled together, building, mixing with something else, something basic and primitive that pulled them closer.

Fire flamed in the depths of his eyes and her body burned from the heat of his skin, so close. His hand tightened around her wrist and she saw the hesitation, the confusion on his face. She thought he'd step back or push her away.

But his mouth crashed against hers, hot, hungry, demanding. She moaned as his tongue plunged into the recesses of her mouth, searching with greedy need. His hand released her wrist and she flattened her palm against his chest, against hard muscle and hot flesh.

His arms came around her waist and pulled her closer, his hands cupping her ass and molding her hips against his body. Another moan escaped her as he pressed the rigid length of his erection against her stomach, rocking against her with a throaty growl she felt clear down to the tips of her toes.

Her hands drifted up to his shoulders, wrapping around his neck. She brushed her fingers through the edge of his hair, surprised at the softness.

He deepened the kiss, the pounding in his chest matching the throbbing in her veins. She leaned in closer, needing to feel more of him, all of him, needing to lose herself.

He dragged his hand up her back, his calloused

palm skimming the flesh as he dragged the hem of her shirt up. His touch was hot, searing, and she moaned again at the sensation, the sound lost in their kiss.

And then he pulled away with a ragged groan, his breathing harsh, heavy. Hooded eyes stared down at her, dazed. He blinked. Looked at her and blinked again.

He pulled his hands away from her body and stepped back, an expression of horror crossing his face before he looked away. Disappointment raced through her as she watched him run his hands over his face, his chest rising and falling with each harsh breath.

She reached behind her, searching for the stool, then slid onto it, a smile lifting her lips when he finally looked at her.

"Jesus Christ. Are you insane?"

She pretended to think about it, then shook her head. "No."

"Really? So you make it a habit of just showing up at some guy's—some *stranger's* house and...and..." He waved his hand between them, unable to finish his sentence. She watched him again, her lips pursed in thought. Then she shook her head.

"Nope, can't say I do. This is pretty much a new one for me."

He ran both hands through his hair, mussing the short length even more, then folded his hands behind his neck and looked up at the ceiling, his lips forming around silent words. CC grabbed the glass of water and took a sip, watching him.

"Why are you really here? And don't tell me it was to drop off my wallet."

She shrugged and put the glass down. "You intrigued me."

"Intrigued? I intrigued you? So you show up at my house and try—" He waved his hand between them again. For some reason, his discomfort and confusion amused her, and she laughed. His eyes narrowed at her and he stepped away, adjusting himself. She didn't even think he realized he did it, which only made her smile more.

"And what the hell would you have done if I hadn't stopped?"

She lowered her gaze pointedly, then looked back up and met his eyes. "Well. I'm hoping I would have enjoyed it. A lot."

*****

PLAYING WITH FIRE

Amber "AJ" Johnson is a freelance writer who has her heart set on becoming a full-time sports reporter at her paper. She has one chance to prove herself: capture an interview with the very private goalie of Baltimore's hockey team, Alec Kolchak. But he's the one man who tries her patience, even as he brings to life a quiet passion she doesn't want to admit exists.

Alec has no desire to be interviewed--he never has, never will. But he finds himself a reluctant admirer of AJ's determination to get what she wants...and he certainly never counted on his attraction to her. In a fit of frustration, he accepts AJ's bet: if she can score just one goal on him in a practice shoot-out, he would not only agree to the interview, he would let her have full access to him for a month, 24/7.

It was a bet neither one of them wanted to lose...and a bet neither one could afford to win. But when it came time to take the shot, could either one of them cross the line?

Forensics accountant Bobbi Reeves is pulled back into a world of shadows in order to go undercover as a personal assistant with the Baltimore Banners. Her assignment: get close to defenseman Nikolai Petrovich and uncover the reason he's being extorted. But she doesn't expect the irrational attraction she feels—or the difficulty in helping someone who doesn't want it.

Nikolai Petrovich, a veteran defenseman for the Banners, has no need for a personal assistant—especially not one hired by the team. During the last eight years, he has learned to live simply...and alone. Experience has taught him that letting people close puts them in danger. He doesn't want a personal assistant, and he certainly doesn't need anyone prying into his personal life. But that doesn't stop his physical reaction to the unusual woman assigned to him.

They are drawn together in spite of their differences, and discover a heated passion that neither expected. But when the game is over, will the secrets they keep pull them closer together...or tear them apart?

Kayli Evans lives a simple life, handling the daily operations of her small family farm and acting as the primary care-taker for her fourteen-year-old niece. She knows the importance of enjoying each minute, of living life to its fullest. But she still has worries: about her older brother's safety in the military, about the rift between her two brothers, and about her niece's security and making ends meet. And now there's a new worry she doesn't want: Ian Donovan, her brother's friend.

Ian is a carefree hockey player for the Baltimore Banners who has relatively few worries—until he finds himself suddenly babysitting his seven-year-old nieces for an extended period of time. He has no idea what he's doing, and is thrust even further into the unknown when he's forced to participate in the twins' newest hobby. Meeting Kayli opens a different world for him, a simpler world where family, trust, and love are what matters most.

Baltimore Banners defenseman Randy Michaels has a reputation for hard-hitting, on and off the ice. But he's getting older, and his agent has warned that there are younger, less-expensive players who are eager to take his place on the team. Can his hare-brained idea of becoming a "respectable businessman" turn his reputation around, or has Randy's reputation really cost him the chance of having his contract renewed?

Alyssa Harris has one goal in mind: make the restaurant she's opened with her three friends a success. It's not going to be easy, not when the restaurant is a themed sports bar geared towards women. It's going to be even more difficult because their sole investor is Randy Michaels, her friend's drool-worthy brother who has his own ideas about what makes an interesting menu.

Will the mismatched pair be able to find a compromise as things heat up, both on and off the ice? Or will their differences result in a penalty that costs both of them the game?

Jean-Pierre "JP" Larocque is a speed demon for the Baltimore Banners. He lives for speed off the ice, too, playing fast and loose with cars and women. But is he really a player, or is his carefree exterior nothing more than a show, hiding a lonely man filled with regret as he struggles to forget the only woman who mattered?

Emily Poole thought she knew what she wanted in life, but everything changed five years ago. Now she exists day by day, helping care for her niece after her sister's bitter divorce. It may not be how she envisioned her life, but she's happy. Or so she thinks, until JP re-enters her life. Now she realizes there's a lot more she wants, including a second chance with JP.

Can these two lost souls finally find forgiveness and Break Away to the future? Or will the shared tragedy of their past tear them apart for good this time?

Valerie Michaels knows all about life, responsibility--and hockey. After all, her brother is a defenseman for the Baltimore Banners. The last thing she needs--or wants--is to get tangled up with one of her brother's teammates. She doesn't have time, not when running The Maypole is her top priority. Could that be the reason she's suddenly drawn to the troubled Justin Tome? Or is it because she senses something deeper inside him, something she thinks she can fix?

On the surface, Justin Tome has it all: a successful career with the Banners, money, fame. But he's been on a downward spiral the last few months. He's become more withdrawn, his game has gone downhill, and he's been partying too much. He thinks it's nothing more than what's expected of him, nothing more than once again failing to meet expectations and never quite measuring up. Then he starts dating Val and realizes that maybe he has more to offer than he thinks.

Or does he? Sometimes voices from the past, voices you've heard all your life, are too strong to overcome. And when the unexpected happens, Justin is certain he's looking at a permanent Delay of Game--unless one strong woman can make him see that life is all about the future, not the past.

Jake Evans has been in the Marine Corps for seventeen years, juggling his conflicting duties to country and his teenage daughter. But when he suffers a serious injury and is sent home, he knows he'll be forced to make decisions he doesn't want to. Battered in spirit and afraid of what the future may hold, he takes the long way by driving cross-country.

He never expected to meet Alyce Marshall, a free-spirited woman on a self-declared adventure: she's running away from home.

In spite of her outward free spirit, Alyce has problems of her own she must face, including the ever-present shadow of her father and his influence on her growing up. She senses similarities in Jake, and decides that it's up to her to teach the tough Marine that life isn't just about rules and regulations. What she doesn't plan on is falling in love with him...and being forced to share her secret.

Michaela Donaldson had her whole life planned out: college, music, and a happy-ever-after with her first true love. One reckless night changed all that, setting Michaela on a new path. Gone are her dreams of pursuing music in college, replaced by what she thinks is a more rewarding life. She's a firefighter now, getting down and dirty while doing her job. So what if she's a little rough around the edges, a little too careless, a little too detached? She's happy, living life on her own terms--until Nicky Lansing shows back up.

Nick Lansing was the stereotypical leather-clad bad boy, needing nothing but his fast car, his guitar, his never-ending partying, and his long-time girlfriend--until one bad decision changed the course of two lives forever. He's on the straight-and-narrow now, living life as a respected teacher and doing his best to be a positive role model. Yes, he still has his music. But gone are his days of partying. And gone is the one girl who always held his heart. Or is she?

One freak accident brings these two opposites back together. Is ten years long enough to heal the physical and emotional wounds from the past? Can they reconcile who they were with who they've become--or will it be a case of Once Burned is enough?

Angie Warren was voted the Most Likely to Succeed in school. She was also voted the Most Responsible. And responsible she is: she made it through college on a scholarship and she's even working her way through Vet School. She has an overprotective older brother she adores and a part-time job tending bar that adds some enjoyment to her life. In fact, that's the only pleasure she has. She's bored and in desperate need of a change. Too bad the one guy she has her sights set on is the one guy completely off-limits.

Jay Moore knows all about excitement and wouldn't live life any other way. From his job as a firefighter to his many brief relationships, his whole life is nothing but one thrilling experience after the other. Except when Angie Warren enters the picture. He's known her for years and there is no way he's going to agree to give her the excitement she's looking for. Even Jay knows where to draw the line—and dating his friend's baby sister definitely crosses all of them.

Too bad Angie has other plans. But will either one of them remember that when you're Playing With Fire, someone is bound to get burned?